MURPHY

Samuel Beckett

MURPHY

GROVE PRESS, INC.   NEW YORK

First Printing, *Collected Works*, 1970

ISBN: 0-394-47517-8
Library of Congress Catalog Card Number: 57-6939

First Printing, Evergreen Edition, 1957
Twentieth Printing 1982
ISBN: 0-394-17210-8
Library of Congress Catalog Card Number: 57-6939

Manufactured in the United States of America

GROVE PRESS, INC., 196 West Houston Street,
New York, N.Y. 10014

MURPHY

1

THE sun shone, having no alternative, on the
nothing new. Murphy sat out of it, as though
he were free, in a mew in West Brompton.
Here for what might have been six months he
had eaten, drunk, slept, and put his clothes on
and off, in a medium-sized cage of north-western
aspect commanding an unbroken view of
medium-sized cages of south-eastern aspect.
Soon he would have to make other arrangements, for the mew had been condemned.
Soon he would have to buckle to and start
eating, drinking, sleeping, and putting his clothes
on and off, in quite alien surroundings.

He sat naked in his rocking-chair of undressed
teak, guaranteed not to crack, warp, shrink, cor-
rode, or creak at night. It was his own, it
never left him. The corner in which he sat was
curtained off from the sun, the poor old sun in

the Virgin again for the billionth time. Seven
scarves held him in position. Two fastened his
shins to the rockers, one his thighs to the seat,
two his breast and belly to the back, one his
wrists to the strut behind. Only the most local
movements were possible. Sweat poured off
him, tightened the thongs. The breath was not
perceptible. The eyes, cold and unwavering
as a gull's, stared up at an iridescence splashed
over the cornice moulding, shrinking and fading. Somewhere a cuckoo-clock, having struck
between twenty and thirty, became the echo
of a street-cry, which now entering the mew
gave *Quid pro quo! Quid pro quo!* directly.

These were sights and sounds that he did
not like. They detained him in the world to
which they belonged, but not he, as he fondly
hoped. He wondered dimly what was breaking
up his sunlight, what wares were being cried.
Dimly, very dimly.

He sat in his chair in this way because it gave
him pleasure! First it gave his body pleasure,
it appeased his body. Then it set him free in
his mind. For it was not until his body was
appeased that he could come alive in his mind,
as described in section six. And life in his mind
gave him pleasure, such pleasure that pleasure
was not the word.

Murphy had lately studied under a man in Cork called Neary. This man, at that time, could stop his heart more or less whenever he liked and keep it stopped, within reasonable limits, for as long as he liked. This rare faculty, acquired after years of application somewhere north of the Nerbudda, he exercised frugally, reserving it for situations irksome beyond endurance, as when he wanted a drink and could not get one, or fell among Gaels and could not escape, or felt the pangs of hopeless sexual inclination.

Murphy's purpose in going to sit at Neary's feet was not to develop the Neary heart, which he thought would quickly prove fatal to a man of his temper, but simply to invest his own with a little of what Neary, at that time a Pythagorean, called the Apmonia. For Murphy had such an irrational heart that no physician could get to the root of it. Inspected, palpated, auscultated, percussed, radiographed and cardiographed, it was all that a heart should be. Buttoned up and left to perform, it was like Petrouchka in his box. One moment in such labour that it seemed on the point of seizing, the next in such ebullition that it seemed on the point of bursting. It was the mediation between these extremes that Neary called the Apmonia. When he got tired of calling it the Apmonia he called it the Isonomy. When he got sick of the sound of Isonomy he called it the Attunement. But he might call it what he liked, into Murphy's heart it would not enter. Neary could not blend the opposites in Murphy's heart.

Their farewell was memorable. Neary came out of one of his dead sleeps and said :

" Murphy, all life is figure and ground."

" But a wandering to find home," said Murphy.

" The face," said Neary, " or system of faces, against the big blooming buzzing confusion. I think of Miss Dwyer."

Murphy could have thought of a Miss Counihan. Neary clenched his fists and raised them before his face.

" To gain the affections of Miss Dwyer," he said, " even for one short hour, would benefit me no end."

The knuckles stood out white under the skin in the usual way—that was the position. The hands then opened quite correctly to the utmost limit of their compass—that was the negation. It now seemed to Murphy that there were two equally legitimate ways in which the gesture might be concluded, and the sublation effected. The hands might be clapped to the head in a

smart gesture of despair, or let fall limply to the
seams of the trousers, supposing that to have
been their point of departure. Judge then of his
annoyance when Neary clenched them again
more violently than before and dashed them
against his breast-bone.

" Half an hour," he said, " fifteen minutes."

" And then ? " said Murphy. " Back to Tene-
riffe and the apes ? "

" You may sneer," said Neary, " and you may
scoff, but the fact remains that all is dross, for
the moment at any rate, that is not Miss Dwyer.
The one closed figure in the waste without
form, and void ! My tetrakyt ! "

Of such was Neary's love for Miss Dwyer, who
loved a Flight-Lieutenant Elliman, who loved a
Miss Farren of Ringsakiddy, who loved a Father
Fitt of Ballinclashet, who in all sincerity was
bound to acknowledge a certain vocation for a
Mrs. West of Passage, who loved Neary.

" Love requited," said Neary, " is a short
circuit," a ball that gave rise to a sparkling
rally.

" The love that lifts up its eyes," said Neary,
" being in torments ; that craves for the tip of
her little finger, dipped in lacquer, to cool its
tongue—is foreign to you, Murphy, I take it."

" Greek," said Murphy.

" Or put it another way," said Neary ; " the single, brilliant, organised, compact blotch in the tumult of heterogeneous stimulation."

" Blotch is the word," said Murphy.

" Just so," said Neary. " Now pay attention to this. For whatever reason you cannot love—— But there is a Miss Counihan, Murphy, is there not ? "

There was indeed a Miss Counihan.

" Now say you were invited to define let us say your commerce with this Miss Counihan, Murphy," said Neary. " Come now, Murphy."

" Precordial," said Murphy, " rather than cordial. Tired. Cork County. Depraved."

" Just so," said Neary. " Now then. For whatever reason you cannot love in my way, and believe me there is no other, for that same reason, whatever it may be, your heart is as it is. And again for that same reason——"

" Whatever it may be," said Murphy.

" I can do nothing for you," said Neary.

" God bless my soul," said Murphy.

" Just so," said Neary. " I should say your conarium has shrunk to nothing."

He worked up the chair to its maximum rock, then relaxed. Slowly the world died down, the big world where *Quid pro quo* was cried as wares

and the light never waned the same way twice ;
in favour of the little, as described in section
six, where he could love himself.

A foot from his ear the telephone burst into
its rail. He had neglected to take down the
receiver. If he did not answer it at once his
landlady would come running to do so, or
some other lodger. Then he would be discovered, for his door was not locked. There
was no means of locking his door. It was a
strange room, the door hanging off its hinges,
and yet a telephone. But its last occupant had
been a harlot, long past her best, which had
been scarlet. The telephone that she had
found useful in her prime, in her decline she
found indispensable. For the only money she
made was when a client from the old days
rang her up. Then she was indemnified for
having been put to unnecessary inconvenience.

Murphy could not free his hand. Every
moment he expected to hear the urgent step of
his landlady on the stairs, or of some other
lodger. The loud calm crake of the telephone
mocked him. At last he freed a hand and seized
the receiver, which in his agitation he clapped
to his head instead of dashing to the ground.

" God blast you," he said.

" He is doing so," she replied. Celia.

He laid the receiver hastily in his lap. The part of him that he hated craved for Celia, the part that he loved shrivelled up at the thought of her. The voice lamented faintly against his flesh. He bore it for a little, then took up the receiver and said :

" Are you never coming back ? "

" I have it," she said.

" Don't I know," said Murphy.

" I don't mean that," she said, " I mean what you told me——"

" I know what you mean," said Murphy.

" Meet me at the usual at the usual," she said. " I'll have it with me."

" That is not possible," said Murphy. " I expect a friend."

" You have no friends," said Celia.

" Well," said Murphy, " not exactly a friend, a funny old chap I ran into."

" You can get rid of him before then," said Celia.

" That is not possible," said Murphy.

" Then I'll bring it round," said Celia.

" You mustn't do that," said Murphy.

" Why don't you want to see me ? " said Celia.

" How often have I to tell you," said Murphy, " I——"

" Listen to me," said Celia. " I don't believe in your funny old chap. There isn't any such animal."

Murphy said nothing. The self that he tried to love was tired.

" I'll be with you at nine," said Celia, " and I'll have it with me. If you're not there——"

" Yes," said Murphy. " Suppose I have to go out ? "

" Good-bye."

He listened for a little to the dead line, he dropped the receiver on the floor, he fastened his hand back to the strut, he worked up the chair. Slowly he felt better, astir in his mind, in the freedom of that light and dark that did not clash, nor alternate, nor fade nor lighten except to their communion, as described in section six. The rock got faster and faster, shorter and shorter, the iridescence was gone, the cry in the mew was gone, soon his body would be quiet. Most things under the moon got slower and slower and then stopped, a rock got faster and faster and then stopped. Soon his body would be quiet, soon he would be free.

2

Age.	Unimportant.
Head.	Small and round.
Eyes.	Green.
Complexion.	White.
Hair.	Yellow.
Features.	Mobile.
Neck.	$13\frac{3}{4}''$.
Upper arm.	$11''$.
Forearm.	$9\frac{1}{2}''$.
Wrist.	$6''$.
Bust.	$34''$.
Waist.	$27''$.
Hips, etc.	$35''$.
Thigh.	$21\frac{3}{4}''$.
Knee.	$13\frac{3}{4}''$.
Calf.	$13''$.
Ankle.	$8\frac{1}{4}''$.
Instep.	Unimportant.
Height.	$5'\ 4''$.
Weight.	123 lbs.

She stormed away from the callbox, accompanied delightedly by her hips, etc. The fiery darts encompassing her about of the amorously disposed were quenched as tow. She entered the saloon bar of a Chef and Brewer and had a sandwich of prawn and tomato and a dock glass of white port off the zinc. She then made her way rapidly on foot, followed by four football pool collectors at four shillings in the pound commission, to the apartment in Tyburnia of her paternal grandfather, Mr. Willoughby Kelly. She kept nothing from Mr. Kelly except what she thought might give him pain, i.e. next to nothing.

She had left Ireland at the age of four.

Mr. Kelly's face was narrow and profoundly seamed with a lifetime of dingy, stingy repose. Just as all hope seemed lost it burst into a fine bulb of skull, unobscured by hair. Yet a little while and his brain-body ratio would have sunk to that of a small bird. He lay back in bed, doing nothing, unless an occasional pluck at the counterpane be entered to his credit.

" You are all I have in the world," said Celia.

Mr. Kelly nestled.

" You," said Celia, " and possibly Murphy."

Mr. Kelly started up in the bed. His eyes could not very well protrude, so deeply were they imbedded, but they could open, and this they did.

" I have not spoken to you of Murphy," said Celia, " because I thought it might give you pain."

" Pain my rump," said Mr. Kelly.

Mr. Kelly fell back in the bed, which closed his eyes, as though he were a doll. He desired Celia to sit down, but she preferred to pace to and fro, clasping and unclasping her hands, in the usual manner. The friendship of a pair of hands.

Celia's account, expurgated, accelerated, improved and reduced, of how she came to have to speak of Murphy, gives the following.

When her parents, Mr. and Mrs. Quentin Kelly died, which they did clinging warmly to their respective partners in the ill-fated *Morro Castle*, Celia, being an only child, went on the street. While this was a step to which Mr. Willoughby Kelly could not whole-heartedly subscribe, yet he did not attempt to dissuade her. She was a good girl, she would do well.

It was on the street, the previous midsummer's night, the sun being then in the Crab, that she met Murphy. She had turned out of Edith Grove into Cremorne Road, intending to refresh herself with a smell of the Reach and then return by Lot's Road, when chancing to glance to her right she saw, motionless in the mouth of Stadium

Street, considering alternately the sky and a sheet of paper, a man. Murphy.

" But I beseech you," said Mr. Kelly, " be less beastly circumstantial. The junction for example of Edith Grove, Cremorne Road and Stadium Street, is indifferent to me. Get up to your man."

She halted—" Get away ! " said Mr. Kelly— set herself off in the line that his eyes must take on their next declension and waited. When his head moved at last, it was to fall with such abandon on his breast that he caught and lost sight of her simultaneously. He did not imme- diately hoist it back to the level at which she could be assessed in comfort, but occupied himself with his sheet. If on his eyes' way back to the eternities she were still in position, he would bid them stay and assess her.

" How do you know all this ? " said Mr. Kelly.

" What ? " said Celia.

" All these demented particulars," said Mr. Kelly.

" He tells me everything," said Celia.

" Lay off them," said Mr. Kelly. " Get up to your man."

When Murphy had found what he sought on the sheet he despatched his head on its upward journey. Clearly the effort was considerable. A little short of half way, grateful for the breather, he arrested the movement and gazed at Celia. For perhaps two minutes she suffered this gladly, then with outstretched arms began slowly to rotate—" Brava ! " said Mr. Kelly— like the Roussel dummy in Regent Street. When she came full circle she found, as she had fully expected, the eyes of Murphy still open and upon her. But almost at once they closed, as for a supreme exertion, the jaws clenched, the chin jutted, the knees sagged, the hypogastrium came forward, the mouth opened, the head tilted slowly back. Murphy was returning to the brightness of the firmament.

Celia's course was clear : the water. The temptation to enter it was strong, but she set it aside. There would be time for that. She walked to a point about half-way between the Battersea and Albert Bridges and sat down on a bench between a Chelsea pensioner and an Eldorado hokey-pokey man, who had dismounted from his cruel machine and was enjoying a short interlude in paradise. Artists of every kind, writers, underwriters, devils, ghosts, columnists, musicians, lyricists, organists, painters and decorators, sculptors and statuaries, critics and reviewers, major and minor, drunk and sober, laughing and crying, in schools and singly, passed up and down. A flotilla of barges, heaped high with waste paper of many colours, riding at anchor or aground on the mud, waved to her from across the water. A funnel vailed to Battersea Bridge. A tug and barge, coupled abreast, foamed happily out of the Reach. The Eldorado man slept in a heap, the Chelsea pensioner tore at his scarlet tunic, exclaiming : " Hell roast this weather, I shill niver fergit it." The clock of Chelsea Old Church ground out grudgingly the hour of ten. Celia rose and walked back the way she had come. But instead of keeping straight on into Lot's Road, as she had hoped, she found herself dragged to the right into Cremorne Road. He was still in the mouth of Stadium Street, in a modified attitude.

" Hell roast this story," said Mr. Kelly, " I shall never remember it."

Murphy had crossed his legs, pocketed his hands, dropped the sheet and was staring straight before him. Celia now accosted him in form— " Wretched girl ! " said Mr. Kelly—whereupon they walked off happily arm-in-arm, leaving the star chart for June lying in the gutter.

" This is where we put on the light," said Mr. Kelly.

Celia put on the light and turned Mr. Kelly's pillows.

From that time forward they were indispensable the one to the other.

" Hey ! " exclaimed Mr. Kelly, " don't skip about like that, will you? You walked away happily arm-in-arm. What happened then ? "

Celia loved Murphy, Murphy loved Celia, it was a striking case of love requited. It dated from that first long lingering look exchanged in the mouth of Stadium Street, not from their walking away arm-in-arm nor any subsequent accident. It was the condition of their walking away, etc., as Murphy had shown her many times in Barbara, Baccardi and Baroko, though never in Bramantip. Every moment that Celia spent away from Murphy seemed an eternity devoid of significance, and Murphy for his part expressed the same thought if possible more strongly in the words : " What is my life now but Celia ? "

On the following Sunday, the moon being at conjunction, he proposed to her in the Battersea Park sub-tropical garden, immediately following the ringing of the bell.

Mr. Kelly groaned.

Celia accepted.

" Wretched girl," said Mr. Kelly, " most wretched."

Resting on Campanella's *City of the Sun*,
Murphy said they must get married by hook or
by crook before the moon came into opposition.
Now it was September, the sun was back in the
Virgin, and their relationship had not yet been
regularised.

Mr. Kelly saw no reason why he should contain
himself any longer. He started up in the bed,
which opened his eyes, as he knew perfectly well
it would, and wanted to know the who, what,
where, by what means, why, in what way and
when. Scratch an old man and find a Quintilian.

" Who is this Murphy," he cried, " for whom
you have been neglecting your work, as I presume ? What is he ? Where does he come
from ? What is his family ? What does he do ?
Has he any money ? Has he any prospects ?
Has he any retrospects ? Is he, has he, anything at all ? "

Taking the first point first, Celia replied that
Murphy was Murphy. Continuing then in an
orderly manner she revealed that he belonged
to no profession or trade ; came from Dublin—
" My God ! " said Mr. Kelly—knew of one
uncle, a Mr. Quigley, a well-to-do ne'er-do-well,
resident in Holland, with whom he strove to
correspond ; did nothing that she could discern ;
sometimes had the price of a concert ; believed

that the future held great things in store for him ;
and never ripped up old stories. He was
Murphy. He had Celia.

Mr. Kelly mustered all his hormones.

" What does he live on ? " he shrieked.

" Small charitable sums," said Celia.

Mr. Kelly fell back. His bolt was shot. The
heavens were free to fall.

Celia now came to that part of her relation
which she rather despaired of explaining to Mr.
Kelly, because she did not properly understand
it herself. She knew that if by any means she
could insert the problem into that immense
cerebrum, the solution would be returned as
though by clockwork. Pacing to and fro at a
slightly faster rate, racking her brain which was
not very large for the best way to say it, she felt
she had come to an even more crucial junction
in her affairs than that composed by Edith
Grove, Cremorne Road and Stadium Street.

" You are all I have in the world," she said.

" I," said Mr. Kelly, " and possibly Murphy."

" There is no one else in the world," said
Celia, " least of all Murphy, that I could speak
to of this."

" You mollify me," said Mr. Kelly.

Celia halted, raised her clasped hands though
she knew his eyes were closed and said :

" Will you please pay attention to this, tell me what it means and what I am to do ? "

" Stop ! " said Mr. Kelly. His attention could not be mobilised like that at a moment's notice. His attention was dispersed. Part was with its caecum, which was wagging its tail again ; part with his extremities, which were dragging anchor ; part with his boyhood ; and so on. All this would have to be called in. When he felt enough had been scraped together he said :

" Go ! "

Celia spent every penny she earned and Murphy earned no pennies. His honourable independence was based on an understanding with his landlady, in pursuance of which she sent exquisitely cooked accounts to Mr. Quigley and handed over the difference, less a reasonable commission, to Murphy. This superb arrangement enabled him to consume away at pretty well his own gait, but was inadequate for a domestic establishment, no matter how frugal. The position was further complicated by the shadows of a clearance area having fallen, not so much on Murphy's abode as on Murphy's landlady. And it was certain that the least appeal to Mr. Quigley would be severely punished. " Shall I bite the hand that starves me," said Murphy, " to have it throttle me ? "

Surely between them they could contrive to earn a little. Murphy thought so, with a look of such filthy intelligence as left her, self-aghast, needing him still. Murphy's respect for the imponderables of personality was profound, he took the miscarriage of his tribute very nicely. If she felt she could not, why then she could not, and that was all. Liberal to a fault, that was Murphy.

" So far I keep abreast," said Mr. Kelly. " There is just this tribute——"

" I have tried so hard to understand that," said Celia.

" But what makes you think a tribute was intended ? " said Mr. Kelly.

" I tell you he keeps nothing from me," said Celia.

" Did it go something like this ? " said Mr. Kelly. " ' I pay you the highest tribute that a man can pay a woman, and you throw a scene.' "

" Hark to the wind," said Celia.

" Damn your eyes," said Mr. Kelly, " did he or didn't he ? "

" It's not a bad guess," said Celia.

" Guess my rump," said Mr. Kelly. " It is the formula."

" So long as one of us understands," said Celia.

In respecting what he called the Archeus,

Murphy did no more than as he would be done by. He was consequently aggrieved when Celia suggested that he might try his hand at something more remunerative than apperceiving himself into a glorious grave and checking the starry concave, and would not take the anguish on his face for an answer. " Did I press you ? " he said. " No. Do you press me ? Yes. Is that equitable ? My sweet."

" Will you conclude now as rapidly as possible," said Mr. Kelly. " I weary of Murphy."

He begged her to believe him when he said he could not earn. Had he not already sunk a small fortune in attempts to do so ? He begged her to believe that he was a chronic emeritus. But it was not altogether a question of economy. There were metaphysical considerations, in whose gloom it appeared that the night had come in which no Murphy could work. Was Ixion under any contract to keep his wheel in nice running order ? Had any provision been made for Tantalus to eat salt ? Not that Murphy had ever heard of.

" But we cannot go on without any money," said Celia.

" Providence will provide," said Murphy.

The imperturbable negligence of Providence to provide goaded them to such transports as

West Brompton had not known since the Earl's Court Exhibition. They said little. Sometimes Murphy would begin to make a point, sometimes he may have even finished making one, it was hard to say. For example, early one morning he said : " The hireling fleeth because he is an hireling." Was that a point ? And again : " What shall a man give in exchange for Celia ? " Was that a point ?

" Those were points undoubtedly," said Mr. Kelly.

When there was no money left and no bill to be cooked for another week, Celia said that either Murphy got work or she left him and went back to hers. Murphy said work would be the end of them both.

" Points one and two," said Mr. Kelly.

Celia had not been long back on the street when Murphy wrote imploring her to return. She telephoned to say that she would return if he undertook to look for work. Otherwise it was useless. He rang off while she was still speaking. Then he wrote again saying he was starved out and would do as she wished. But as there was no possibility of his finding in himself any reason for work taking one form rather than another, would she kindly procure a corpus of incentives based on the only system outside his own in which he felt the least confidence, that of the heavenly bodies. In Berwick Market there was a swami who cast excellent nativities for sixpence. She knew the year and date of the unhappy event, the time did not matter. The science that had got over Jacob and Esau would not insist on the precise moment of vagitus. He would attend to the matter himself, were it not that he was down to fourpence.

"And now I ring him up," concluded Celia, "to tell him I have it, and he tries to choke me off."

"It?" said Mr. Kelly.

"What he told me to get," said Celia.

"Are you afraid to call it by its name?" said Mr. Kelly.

"That is all," said Celia. "Now tell me what to do, because I have to go."

Drawing himself up for the third time in the bed Mr. Kelly said:

"Approach, my child."

Celia sat down on the edge of the bed, their four hands mingled on the counterpane, they gazed at one another in silence.

"You are crying, my child," said Mr. Kelly. Not a thing escaped him.

"How can a person love you and go on

like that?" said Celia. "Tell me how it is possible."

"He is saying the same about you," said Mr. Kelly.

"To his funny old chap," said Celia.

"I beg your pardon," said Mr. Kelly.

"No matter," said Celia. "Hurry up and tell me what to do."

"Approach, my child," said Mr. Kelly, slipping away a little from his surroundings.

"Damn it, I am approached," said Celia. "Do you want me to get in beside you?"

The blue glitter of Mr. Kelly's eyes in the uttermost depths of their orbits became fixed, then veiled by the classical pythonic glaze. He raised his left hand, where Celia's tears had not yet dried, and seated it pronate on the crown of his skull—that was the position. In vain. He raised his right hand and laid the forefinger along his nose. He then returned both hands to their point of departure with Celia's on the counterpane, the glitter came back into his eye and he pronounced:

"Chuck him."

Celia made to rise, Mr. Kelly pinioned her wrists.

"Sever your connexion with this Murphy," he said, "before it is too late."

" Let me go," said Celia.

" Terminate an intercourse that must prove fatal," he said, " while there is yet time."

" Let me go," said Celia.

He let her go and she stood up. They gazed at each other in silence. Mr. Kelly missed nothing, his seams began to work.

" I bow to passion," he said.

Celia went to the door.

" Before you go," said Mr. Kelly, " you might hand me the tail of my kite. Some tassels have come adrift."

Celia went to the cupboard where he kept his kite, took out the tail and loose tassels and brought them over to the bed.

" As you say," said Mr. Kelly, " hark to the wind. I shall fly her out of sight to-morrow."

He fumbled vaguely at the coils of tail. Already he was in position, straining his eyes for the speck that was he, digging in his heels against the immense pull skyward. Celia kissed him and left him.

" God willing," said Mr. Kelly, " right out of sight."

Now I have no one, thought Celia, except possibly Murphy.

3

THE moon, by a striking coincidence full and at
perigee, was 29,000 miles nearer the earth than
it had been for four years. Exceptional tides
were expected. The Port of London Authority
was calm.

It was after ten when Celia reached the mew.
There was no light in his window, but that did
not trouble her, who knew how addicted he was
to the dark. She had raised her hand to knock
the knock that he knew, when the door flew open
and a man smelling strongly of drink rattled past
her down the steps. There was only one way
out of the mew, and this he took after a brief
hesitation. He spurned the ground behind him
in a spring-heeled manner, as though he longed
to run but did not dare. She entered the house,
her mind still tingling with the clash of his leaden
face and scarlet muffler, and switched on the
light in the passage. In vain, the bulb had been
taken away. She started to climb the stairs in
the dark. On the landing she paused to give

herself a last chance, Murphy and herself a last chance.

She had not seen him since the day he stigmatised work as the end of them both, and now she came creeping upon him in the dark to execute a fake jossy's sixpenny writ to success and prosperity. He would be thinking of her as a Fury coming to carry him off, or even as a tipstaff with warrant to distrain. Yet it was not she, but Love, that was the bailiff. She was but the bumbailiff. This discrimination gave her such comfort that she sat down on the stairhead, in the pitch darkness excluding the usual auspices. How different it had been on the riverside, when the barges had waved, the funnel bowed, the tug and barge sung, yes to her. Or had they meant no? The distinction was so nice. What difference, for example, would it make now, whether she went on up the stairs to Murphy or back down them into the mew? The difference between her way of destroying them both, according to him, and his way, according to her. The gentle passion.

No sound came from Murphy's room, but that did not trouble her, who knew how addicted he was to remaining still for long periods.

She fumbled in her bag for a coin. If her thumb felt the head she would go up; if her

devil's finger, down. Her devil's finger felt the
head and she rose to depart. An appalling
sound issued from Murphy's room, a flurry of
such despairing quality that she dropped the
bag, followed after a short silence by a suspira-
tion more lamentable than any groan. For a
moment she did not move, the power to do so
having deserted her. No sooner did this return
than she snatched up the bag and flew to the
rescue, as she supposed. Thus the omen of the
coin was overruled.

Murphy was as last heard of, with this
difference however, that the rocking-chair was
now on top. Thus inverted his only direct
contact with the floor was that made by his
face, which was ground against it. His attitude
roughly speaking was that of a very inexperienced
diver about to enter the water, except that his
arms were not extended to break the concussion,
but fastened behind him. Only the most local
movements were possible, a licking of the lips, a
turning of the other cheek to the dust, and so on.
Blood gushed from his nose.

Losing no time in idle speculation Celia undid
the scarves and prised the chair off him with all
possible speed. Part by part he subsided, as the
bonds that held him fell away, until he lay
fully prostrate in the crucified position, heaving.

A huge pink nævus on the pinnacle of the right buttock held her spellbound. She could not understand how she had never noticed it before.

" Help," said Murphy.

Startled from her reverie she set to and rendered him every form of assistance known to an old Girl Guide. When she could think of nothing more she dragged him out of the corner, shovelled the rocking-chair under him, emptied him on to the bed, laid him out decently, covered him with a sheet and sat down beside him. The next move was his.

" Who are you? " said Murphy.

Celia mentioned her name. Murphy, unable to believe his ears, opened his eyes. The beloved features emerging from chaos were the face against the big blooming buzzing confusion of which Neary had spoken so highly. He closed his eyes and opened his arms. She sank down athwart his breast, their heads were side by side on the pillow but facing opposite ways, his fingers strayed through her yellow hair. It was the short circuit so earnestly desired by Neary, the glare of pursuit and flight extinguished.

In the morning he described in simple language how he came to be in that extraordinary position. Having gone to sleep, though sleep was hardly the word, in the chair, the next thing was he was having a heart attack. When this happened when he was normally in bed, nine times out of ten his struggles to subdue it landed him on the floor. It was therefore not surprising, given his trussed condition, that on this occasion they had caused the entire machine to turn turtle.

" But who tied you up ? " said Celia.

She knew nothing of this recreation, in which Murphy had not felt the need to indulge while she was with him. He now gave her a full and frank account of its unique features.

" I was just getting it going when you rang up," he said.

Nor did she know anything of his heart attacks, which had not troubled him while she was with him. He now told her all about them, keeping back nothing that might alarm her.

" So you see," he said, " what a difference your staying with me makes."

Celia turned her face to the window. Clouds were moving rapidly across the sky. Mr. Kelly would be crowing.

" My bag is on the floor your side," she said.

The fall on the landing had cracked the mirror set in the flap. She stifled a cry, averted her head and handed him a large black envelope with the title in letters of various colours.

"What you told me to get," she said.

She felt him take it from her. When after some little time he still had not spoken nor made any movement she turned her head to see was anything amiss. All the colour (yellow) had ebbed from his face, leaving it ashen. A pale strand of blood scoring the jaw illustrated this neap. He kept her waiting a little longer and then said, in a voice unfamiliar to her :

"My life-warrant. Thank you."

It struck her that a merely indolent man would not be so affected by the prospect of employment.

"My little bull of incommunication," he said, "signed not with lead but with a jossy's spittle. Thank you."

Celia, hardening her heart, passed him a hairpin. Murphy's instinct was to treat this dun as he had those showered upon him in the days when he used to enjoy an income, namely, steam it open, marvel at its extravagance and return it undelivered. But then he had not been in bed with the collector.

"Why the black envelope," she said, "and the different-coloured letters ? "

"Because Mercury," said Murphy, "god of thieves, planet *par excellence* and mine, has no fixed colour." He spread out the sheet folded in sixteen. "And because this is blackmail."

THEMA COELI

With Delineations
Compiled

By

RAMASWAMI KRISHNASWAMI NARAYANASWAMI SUK

Genethliac
Famous throughout Civilised World and Irish Free State

" *Then I defy you, Stars.*"

THE GOAT

At time of Birth of this Native four degrees of the GOAT was rising, his highest attributes being Soul, Emotion, Clairaudience and Silence. Few Minds are better concocted than this Native's.

The Moon twenty-three degrees of the Serpent promotes great Magical Ability of the Eye, to which the lunatic would easy succumb. Avoid exhaustion by speech. Intense Love nature prominent, rarely suspicioning the Nasty, with inclinations to Purity. When Sensuality rules there is danger of Fits.

Mars having just set in the East denotes a great desire to engage in some pursuit, yet not. There has been persons of this description known to have expressed a wish to be in two places at a time.

When Health is below par, Regret may be entertained. May be termed a law-abiding character having a superior appearance. Should avoid drugs and resort to Harmony. Great care should be used in dealing with publishers, quadrupeds and tropical swamps, as these may terminate unprofitably for the Native.

Mercury sesquiquadrate with the Anarete is most malefic and will greatly conduce to Success terminating in the height of Glory, which may injure Native's prospects.

The Square of Moon and Solar Orb afflicts the Hyleg. Herschel in Aquarius stops the Water and he should guard against this. Neptune and Venus in the Bull denotes dealings with the Females only medium developed or of low organic quality. Companions or matrimonial Mate are recommended to be born under a fiery triplicity, when the Bowman should permit of a small family.

With regards to a Career, the Native should inspire and lead, as go between, promoter, detective, custodian, pioneer or, if possible, explorer, his motto in business being large profits and a quick turnover.

The Native should guard against Bright's disease and Grave's disease, also pains in the neck and feet.

Lucky Gems. Amethyst and Diamond. To ensure Success the Native should sport.

Lucky Colours. Lemon. To avert Calamity the Native should have a dash in apparel, also a squeeze in home decorations.

Lucky Days. Sunday. To attract the maximum Success the Native should begin new ventures.

Lucky Numbers. 4. The Native should commence new enterprises, for in so doing lies just that difference between Success and Calamity.

Lucky Years. 1936 and 1990. Successful and prosperous, though not without calamities and setbacks.

" Is it even so," said Murphy, his yellow all

revived by these prognostications. " Pandit Suk has never done anything better."

" Can you work now after that ? " said Celia.

" Certainly I can," said Murphy. " The very first fourth to fall on a Sunday in 1936 I begin. I put on my gems and off I go, to custode, detect, explore, pioneer, promote or pimp, as occasion may arise."

" And in the meantime ? " said Celia.

" In the meantime," said Murphy, " I must just watch out for fits, publishers, quadrupeds, the stone, Bright's——"

She gave a cry of despair intense while it lasted, then finished and done with, like an infant's.

" How you can be such a fool and a brute," she said, and did not bother to finish.

" But you wouldn't have me go against the diagram," said Murphy, " surely to God."

" A fool and a brute," she said.

" Surely that is rather severe," said Murphy.

" You tell me to get you this . . . this . . ."

" Corpus of deterrents," said Murphy.

" So that we can be together, and then you go and twist it into a . . . into a . . ."

" Separation order," said Murphy. Few minds were better concocted than this native's.

Celia opened her mouth to proceed, closed

it without having done so. She despatched her hands on the gesture that Neary had made such a botch of at the thought of Miss Dwyer, and resolved it quite legitimately, as it seemed to Murphy, by dropping them back into their original position. Now she had nobody, except possibly Mr. Kelly. She again opened and closed her mouth, then began the slow business of going.

" You are not going," said Murphy.

" Before I'm kicked out," said Celia.

" But what is the good of going merely in body ? " said Murphy, thereby giving the conversation a twist that brought it within her powers of comment.

" You are too modest," she said.

" Oh, do not let us fence," said Murphy, " at least let it never be said that we fenced."

" I go as best I can," she said, " the same as I went last time."

It really did look as though she were going, at her present rate of adjustment she would be gone in twenty minutes or half an hour. Already she was at work on her face.

" I won't come back," she said. " I won't open your letters. I'll move my pitch."

Convinced he had hardened his heart and would let her go, she was taking her time.

"I'll be sorry I met you," she said.

"*Met* me!" said Murphy. "Met is magnificent."

He thought it wiser not to capitulate until it was certain that she would not. In the meantime, what about a small outburst. It could do no harm, it might do good. He did not feel really up to it, he knew that long before the end he would wish he had not begun. But it was perhaps better than lying there silent, watching her lick her lips, and waiting. He launched out.

"This love with a function gives me a pain in the neck——"

"Not in the feet?" said Celia.

"What do you love?" said Murphy. "Me as I am. You can want what does not exist, you can't love it." This came well from Murphy. "Then why are you all out to change me? So that you won't have to love me," the voice rising here to a note that did him credit, "so that you won't be condemned to love me, so that you'll be reprieved from loving me." He was anxious to make his meaning clear. "Women are all the same bloody same, you can't love, you can't stay the course, the only feeling you can stand is being felt, you can't love for five minutes without wanting it abolished in brats and house bloody wifery. My God, how I hate the charVenus and her sausage and mash sex."

Celia put a foot to the ground.

" Avoid exhaustion by speech," she said.

" Have I wanted to change you? Have I pestered you to begin things that don't belong to you and stop things that do? How can I care what you DO?"

" I am what I do," said Celia.

" No," said Murphy. " You do what you are, you do a fraction of what you are, you suffer a dreary ooze of your being into doing." He threw his voice into an infant's whinge. " ' I cudden do annytting, Maaaammy.' That kind of doing. Unavoidable and tedious."

Celia was now fully seated on the edge of the bed, her back turned to him, making fast her Bollitoes.

" I have heard bilge," she said, and did not bother to finish.

" Hear a little more," said Murphy, " and then I expire. If I had to work out what you are from what you do, you could skip out of here now and joy be with you. First of all you starve me into terms that are all yours but the jossy, then you won't abide by them. The arrangement is that I enter the jaws of a job according to the celestial prescriptions of Professor Suk, then when I won't go against them you start to walk out on me. Is that the way you respect an agreement? What more can I do?"

He closed his eyes and fell back. It was not his habit to make out cases for himself. An atheist chipping the deity was not more senseless than Murphy defending his courses of inaction, as he did not require to be told. He had been carried away by his passion for Celia and by a most curious feeling that he should not collapse without at least the form of a struggle. This grisly relic from the days of nuts, balls and sparrows astonished himself. To die fighting was the perfect antithesis of his whole practice, faith and intention.

He heard her rise and go to the window, then come and stand at the foot of the bed. So far from opening his eyes he sucked in his cheeks. Was she perhaps subject to feelings of compassion?

" I'll tell you what more you can do," she said. " You can get up out of that bed, make yourself decent and walk the streets for work."

The gentle passion. Murphy lost all his yellow again.

"The streets!" he murmured. "Father forgive her."

He heard her go to the door.

"Not the slightest idea," he murmured, "of what her words mean. No more insight into their implications than a parrot into its profanities."

As he seemed likely to go on mumbling and marvelling to himself for some time, Celia said good-bye and opened the door.

"You don't know what you are saying," said Murphy. "Let me tell you what you are saying. Close the door."

Celia closed the door but kept her hand on the handle.

"Sit on the bed," said Murphy.

"No," said Celia.

"I can't talk against space," said Murphy, "my fourth highest attribute is silence. Sit on the bed."

The tone was that adopted by exhibitionists for their last words on earth. Celia sat on the bed. He opened his eyes, cold and unwavering as a gull's, and with great magical ability sunk their shafts into hers, greener than he had ever seen them and more hopeless than he had ever seen anybody's.

"What have I now?" he said. "I distinguish. You, my body and my mind." He paused for this monstrous proposition to be granted. Celia did not hesitate, she might never have occasion to grant him anything again. " In the mercantile gehenna," he said, " to which your words invite me, one of these will go, or two, or all. If you, then you only ; if my body, then you also ; if my mind, then all. Now ? "

She looked at him helplessly. He seemed serious. But he had seemed serious when he spoke of putting on his gems and lemon, etc. She felt, as she felt so often with Murphy, spattered with words that went dead as soon as they sounded ; each word obliterated, before it had time to make sense, by the word that came next ; so that in the end she did not know what had been said. It was like difficult music heard for the first time.

" You twist everything," she said. " Work needn't mean any of that."

" Then is the position unchanged ? " said Murphy. " Either I do what you want or you walk out. Is that it ? "

She made to rise, he pinioned her wrists.

" Let me go," said Celia.

" Is it ? " said Murphy.

" Let me go," said Celia.

He let her go. She rose and went to the window. The sky, cool, bright, full of movement, anointed her eyes, reminded her of Ireland.

"Yes or no?" said Murphy. The eternal tautology.

"Yes," said Celia. "Now you hate me."

"No," said Murphy. "Look is there a clean shirt."

4

In Dublin a week later, that would be September 19th, Neary minus his whiskers was recognised by a former pupil called Wylie, in the General Post Office contemplating from behind the statue of Cuchulain. Neary had bared his head, as though the holy ground meant something to him. Suddenly he flung aside his hat, sprang forward, seized the dying hero by the thighs and began to dash his head against his buttocks, such as they are. The Civic Guard on duty in the building, roused from a tender reverie by the sound of blows, took in the situation at his leisure, disentangled his baton and advanced with measured tread, thinking he had caught a vandal in the act. Happily Wylie, whose reactions as a street bookmaker's stand were as rapid as a zebra's, had already seized Neary round the waist, torn him back from the sacrifice and smuggled him half-way to the exit.

"Howlt on there, youze," said the C.G.

Wylie turned back, tapped his forehead and said, as one sane man to another :

" John o' God's.   Hundred per cent harmless."

" Come back in here owwathat," said the C.G.

Wylie, a tiny man, stood at a loss. Neary, almost as large as the C.G. though not of course so nobly proportioned, rocked blissfully on the right arm of his rescuer. It was not in the C.G.'s nature to bandy words, nor had it come into any branch of his training. He resumed his steady advance.

" Stillorgan," said Wylie.   " Not Dundrum."

The C.G. laid his monstrous hand on Wylie's left arm and exerted a strong pull along the line he had mapped out in his mind. They all moved off in the desired direction, Neary shod with orange-peel.

" John o' God's," said Wylie.   " As quiet as a child."

They drew up behind the statue. A crowd gathered behind them.   The C.G. leaned forward and scrutinised the pillar and draperies.

" Not a feather out of her," said Wylie. " No blood, no brains, nothing."

The C.G. straightened up and let go Wylie's arm.

" Move on," he said to the crowd, " before yer moved on."

The crowd obeyed, with the single diastole-
systole which is all the law requires. Feeling
amply repaid by this superb symbol for the
trouble and risk he had taken in issuing an
order, the C.G. inflected his attention to Wylie
and said more kindly :

" Take my advice, mister——" He stopped.
To devise words of advice was going to tax his
ability to the utmost. When would he learn
not to plunge into the labyrinths of an opinion
when he had not the slightest idea of how he
was to emerge ? And before a hostile audience !
His embarrassment was if possible increased by
the expression of strained attention on Wylie's
face, clamped there by the promise of advice.

" Yes, sergeant," said Wylie, and held his
breath.

" Run him back to Stillorgan," said the C.G.
Done it !

Wylie's face came asunder in gratification.

" Never fear, sergeant," he said, urging Neary
towards the exit, " back to the cell, blood heat,
next best thing to never being born, no heroes,
no fisc, no——"

Neary had been steadily recovering all this
time and now gave such a jerk to Wylie's arm
that that poor little man was nearly pulled off
his feet.

" Where am I ? " said Neary. " If and when."

Wylie rushed him into the street and into a Dalkey tram that had just come in. The crowd dispersed, the better to gather elsewhere. The C.G. dismissed the whole sordid episode from his mind, the better to brood on a theme very near to his heart.

" Is it the saloon," said Neary, " or the jugs and bottles? "

Wylie wet his handkerchief and applied it tenderly to the breaches of surface, a ministration immediately poleaxed by Neary, who now saw his saviour for the first time. Punctured by those sharp little features of the fury that had sustained him, he collapsed in a tempest of sobbing on that sharp little shoulder.

" Come, come," said Wylie, patting the large heaving back. " Needle is at hand."

Neary checked his sobs, raised a face purged of all passion, seized Wylie by the shoulders, held him out at arm's length and exclaimed :

" Is it little Needle Wylie, my scholar that was. What will you have ? "

" How do you feel ? " said Wylie.

It dawned on Neary that he was not where he thought. He rose.

" What is the finest tram in Europe," he said, " to a man consumed with sobriety ? " He made the street under his own power with Wylie close behind him.

"But by Mooney's clock," said Wylie, "the sad news is two-thirty-three."

Neary leaned against the Pillar railings and cursed, first the day in which he was born, then—in a bold flash-back—the night in which he was conceived.

"There, there," said Wylie. "Needle knows no holy hour."

He led the way to an underground café close by, steered Neary into an alcove and called for Cathleen. Cathleen came.

"My friend Professor Neary," said Wylie, "my friend Miss Cathleen na Hennessey."

"Pleased," said Cathleen.

"Why the ——," said Neary, "is light given to a man whose way is hid."

"Pardon," said Cathleen.

"Two large coffees," said Wylie. "Three star."

One gulp of this and Neary's way was clearer.

"Now tell us all about it," said Wylie. "Keep back nothing."

"The limit of Cork endurance had been reached," said Neary. "That Red Branch bum was the camel's back."

"Drink a little more of your coffee," said Wylie.

Neary drank a little more.

" What are you doing in this kip at all ? " said Wylie. " Why aren't you in Cork ? "

" My grove on Grand Parade," said Neary, " is wiped as a man wipeth a plate, wiping it and turning it upside down."

" And your whiskers ? " said Wylie.

" Suppressed without pity," said Neary, " in discharge of a vow, never again to ventilate a virility denied discharge into its predestined channel."

" These are dark sayings," said Wylie.

Neary turned his cup upside down.

" Needle," he said, " as it is with the love of the body, so with the friendship of the mind, the full is only reached by admittance to the most retired places. Here are the pudenda of my psyche."

" Cathleen," cried Wylie.

" But betray me," said Neary, " and you go the way of Hippasos."

" The Akousmatic, I presume," said Wylie. " His retribution slips my mind."

" Drowned in a puddle," said Neary, " for having divulged the incommensurability of side and diagonal."

" So perish all babblers," said Wylie.

" And the construction of the regular dodeca

—hic—dodecahedron," said Neary. " Excuse me."

Neary's account, expurgated, accelerated, improved and reduced, of how he came to reach the end of Cork endurance, gives the following.

No sooner had Miss Dwyer, despairing of recommending herself to Flight-Lieutenant Elliman, made Neary as happy as a man could desire, than she became one with the ground against which she had figured so prettily. Neary wrote to Herr Kurt Koffka demanding an immediate explanation. He had not yet received an answer.

The problem then became how to break with the morsel of chaos without hurting its feelings. The *plaisir de rompre*, for Murphy the rationale of social contacts, was alien to Neary. He insisted, by word and deed, that he was not worthy of her, a hackneyed device that had the desired effect. And it was not long before Miss Dwyer had made Flight-Lieutenant Elliman, despairing of recommending himself to Miss Farren of Ringsakiddy, as happy as a Flight-Lieutenant could desire.

Then Neary met Miss Counihan, in the month of March, ever since when his relation toward her had been that post-mortem of Dives to Lazarus, except that there was no Father Abra-

ham to put in a good word for him. Miss
Counihan was sorry, her breast was preoccupied.
She was touched and flattered, but her affections
were in bond. The happy man, since Neary
would press his breast to the thorn, was Mr.
Murphy, one of his former scholars.

" Holy God ! " said Wylie.

" That long hank of Apollonian asthenia,"
groaned Neary, " that schizoidal spasmophile,
occupying the breast of angel Counihan. Can
such things be ! "

" A notable wet indeed," said Wylie. " He
addressed me once."

" The last time I saw him," said Neary, " he
was saving up for a Drinker artificial respiration
machine to get into when he was fed up breathing."

" He expressed the hope, I remember," said
Wylie, " that I might get safely back to my
bottle of hay before someone found me."

Neary's heart (when not suspended) not only
panted after Miss Counihan, but bled for her
into the bargain, for he was convinced that she
had been abandoned. He recalled how Murphy
had boasted of conducting his amours on the
lines laid down by Fletcher's Sullen Shepherd.
And the terms he had used in speaking of Miss
Counihan did not suggest that he had earmarked
her for special treatment.

Murphy had left the Gymnasium the previous February, about a month before Neary met Miss Counihan. Since then the only news of him was that he had been seen in London on Maundy Thursday late afternoon, supine on the grass in the Cockpit in Hyde Park, alone and plunged in a torpor from which all efforts to rouse him had proved unsuccessful.

Neary besieged Miss Counihan with attentions, sending her mangoes, orchids, Cuban cigarettes and a passionately autographed copy of his tractate, *The Doctrine of the Limit*. If she did not acknowledge these gifts, at least she did not return them, so that Neary continued to hope. Finally she gave him a forenoon appointment at the grave of Father Prout (F. S. Mahony) in Shandon Churchyard, the one place in Cork she knew of where fresh air, privacy and immunity from assault were reconciled.

Neary arrived with a superb bunch of cattleyas, which on her arrival two hours later she took graciously from him and laid on the slab. She then made a statement designed to purge the unhappy man of such remaining designs on her person as he might happen to cherish.

She was set aside for Murphy, who had torn himself away to set up for his princess, in some less desolate quarter of the globe, a habitation meet for her. When he had done this he would come flying back to claim her. She had not heard from him since his departure, and therefore did not know where he was, or what exactly he was doing. This did not disquiet her, as he had explained before he left that to make good and love, were it only by letter, at one and the same time, was more than he could manage. Consequently he would not write until he had some tangible success to report. She would not inflict needless pain on Neary by enlarging on the nature of her feeling for Mr. Murphy, enough had been said to make it clear that she could not tolerate his propositions. If he were not gentleman enough to desist on his own bottom, she would have him legally restrained.

At this point Neary paused and buried his face in his hands.

" My poor friend," said Wylie.

Neary reached forward with his hands across the marble top to Wylie, who seized them in an ecstasy of compassion and began to massage them. Neary closed his eyes. In vain. The human eyelid is not teartight (happily for the human eye). In the presence of such grief Wylie felt purer than at any time since his second communion.

" Do not tell me any more," he said, "if it gives you so much pain."

" Two in distress," said Neary, " make sorrow less."

To free the hand from sympathetic pressure is an operation requiring such an exquisite touch that Neary decided he had better not attempt it. The ruse he adopted so that Wylie might not be wounded was to beg for a cigarette. He went further, he suffered his cup to be replenished.

Miss Counihan, her statement concluded, turned to go. Neary sank on one knee, on both knees, and begged her to hear him in a voice so hoarse with anguish that she turned back.

" Mr. Neary," she said, almost gently, " I am sorry if I have seemed to speak unfeelingly. Believe me, I have nothing against you personally. If I were not—er—disposed of, I might even learn to like you, Mr. Neary. But you must understand that I am not free to—er—do justice to your addresses. Try and forget me, Mr. Neary."

Wylie rubbed his hands.

" Things are looking up," he said.

Again she turned to go, again Neary stayed her, this time with the assurance that what he had to say concerned not himself but Murphy. He described the position in which that knight-errant had last been heard of.

" London! " exclaimed Miss Counihan. " The

Mecca of every young aspirant to fiscal distinction."

This was a balloon that Neary quickly punctured, with a sketch of the phases through which the young aspirant in London had to pass before he could call himself an old suspirant. He then made what he would always regard as the greatest blunder of his career. He began to disparage Murphy.

That afternoon he shaved off his whiskers.

He did not see her again for nearly four months, when she knocked into him skilfully in the Mall. She looked ill (she was ill). It was August and still she had no news of Murphy. Was there no means of getting in touch with him. Neary, who had already gone deeply into this question, replied that he could not think of any. He seemed to have only one person belonging to him, a demented uncle who spent his time between Amsterdam and Scheveningen. Miss Counihan went on to say that she could not very well renounce a young man, such a nice young man, who for all she knew to the contrary was steadily amassing a large fortune so that she might not be without any of the little luxuries to which she was accustomed, and whom of course she loved very dearly, unless she had superlative reasons for doing, such for example

as would flow from a legally attested certificate
of his demise, a repudiation of her person under
his own hand and seal, or overwhelming evidence
of infidelity and economic failure.   She welcomed
the happy chance that allowed her to com-
municate this—er—modified view of the situation to Mr. Neary, looking so much more—er—
youthful without his whiskers, on the very eve of
her departure to Dublin, where Wynn's Hotel
would always find her.

The next morning Neary closed the Gymnasium, put a padlock on the Grove, sunk both
keys in the Lee and boarded the first train for
Dublin, accompanied by his *âme damnée* and man-
of-all-work, Cooper.

Cooper's only visible humane characteristic
was a morbid craving for alcoholic depressant.
So long as he could be kept off the bottle he was
an invaluable servant.   He was a low-sized,
clean-shaven, grey-faced, one-eyed man, trior-
chous and a non-smoker.   He had a curious
hunted walk, like that of a destitute diabetic in a
strange city.   He never sat down and never
took off his hat.

This ruthless tout was now launched in pursuit
of Murphy, with the torpor in the Cockpit as the
only clue.   But many a poor wretch had been
nailed by Cooper with very much less to work

on. While Cooper was combing London, where he would stay at the usual stew, Neary would be working a line of his own in Dublin, where Wynn's Hotel would always find him. When Cooper found Murphy, all he had to do was to notify Neary by wire.

A feature of Miss Counihan's attitude to Neary had been the regularity of its alternation. Having shown herself cruel, kind, cruel and kind in turn, she could no more welcome his arrival at her hotel than green, yellow, green is a legitimate sequence of traffic lights.

Either he left the hotel or she did. He did, so that at least he might know whose were the happy beds and breakfasts. If he attempted to speak to her again before he had equipped himself with the—er—discharge papers aforesaid, she would send for the police.

Neary crawled to the nearest station doss. All depended now on Cooper. If Cooper failed him he would simply post himself early one morning outside her hotel and as soon as she came tripping down the steps take salts of lemon.

In the meantime there was little he could do. He began feebly to look for a thread that might lead him to Murphy among the nobility, tradesmen and gentry of that name in Dublin, but soon left off, appalled. He instructed the hall

porter in Wynn's to send any telegrams addressed
to him from London across the street to Mooney's,
where he would always be found. There he sat
all day, moving slowly from one stool to another
until he had completed the circuit of the counters,
when he would start all over again in the reverse
direction. He did not speak to the curates, he
did not drink the endless half-pints of porter that
he had to buy, he did nothing but move slowly
round the ring of counters, first in one direction,
then in the other, thinking of Miss Counihan.
When the house closed at night he went back to
the doss and dossed, and in the morning he did
not get up until shortly before the house was due
to open. The hour from 2.30 to 3.30 he devoted
to having himself shaved to the pluck. The
whole of Sunday he spent in doss, as the hall
porter at Wynn's was aware, thinking of Miss
Counihan. The power to stop his heart had
deserted him.

" My poor friend," said Wylie.

" Till this morning," said Neary. Feeling his
mouth beginning to twitch he covered it with his
hand. In vain. The face is an organised whole.
" Or rather this afternoon," he said, directly he
was able.

He had reached the turn and was thinking of
ebbing back when the boots from Wynn's came

in and handed him a telegram. FOUND STOP
LOOK SLIPPY STOP COOPER. He was still laughing
and crying, to the great relief of the curates, who
had grown to detest and dread that frozen face
day after day at their counters, when the boots
returned with a second telegram. LOST STOP
STOP WHERE YOU ARE STOP COOPER.

" I have a confused recollection," said Neary,
" of being thrown out."

" The curate mentality," said Wylie.

" Then nothing more," said Neary, " until
that deathless rump was trying to stare me down."

" But there is no rump," said Wylie. " How
could there be ? What chance would a rump
have in the G.P.O. ? "

" I tell you I saw it," said Neary, " trying to
downface me."

Wylie told him what happened next.

" Do not quibble," said Neary harshly. " You
saved my life. Now palliate it."

" I greatly fear," said Wylie, " that the syndrome known as life is too diffuse to admit of
palliation. For every symptom that is eased,
another is made worse. The horse leech's
daughter is a closed system. Her quantum of
wantum cannot vary."

" Very prettily put," said Neary.

" For an example of what I mean," said Wylie,

" you have merely to consider the young Fellow of Trinity College——"

" Merely is excellent," said Neary.

" He sought relief in insulin," said Wylie, " and cured himself of diabetes."

" Poor old chap," said Neary. " Relief from what ? "

" The sweated sinecure," said Wylie.

" I don't wonder at Berkeley," said Neary. " He had no alternative. A defence mechanism. Immaterialise or bust. The sleep of sheer terror. Compare the opossum."

" The advantage of this view," said Wylie, " is, that while one may not look forward to things getting any better, at least one need not fear their getting any worse. They will always be the same as they always were."

" Until the system is dismantled," said Neary.

" Supposing that to be permitted," said Wylie.

" From all of which I am to infer," said Neary, " correct me if I am wrong, that the possession— *Deus det !*—of angel Counihan will create an aching void to the same amount."

" Humanity is a well with two buckets," said Wylie, " one going down to be filled, the other coming up to be emptied."

" What I make on the swings of Miss Counihan," said Neary, " if I understand you, I lose on the roundabouts of the non-Miss Counihan."

" Very prettily put," said Wylie.

" There is no non-Miss Counihan," said Neary.

" There will be," said Wylie.

" Help there to be," cried Neary, clasping his hands, " in this Coney Eastern Island that is Neary, some Chinese attractions other than Miss Counihan."

" Now you are talking," said Wylie. " When you ask for heal-all you are not talking. But when you ask for a single symptom to be superseded, then I am bound to admit that you are talking."

" There is only the one symptom," said Neary. " Miss Counihan."

" Well," said Wylie, " I do not think we should have much difficulty in finding a substitute."

" I declare to my God," said Neary, " sometimes you talk as great tripe as Murphy."

" Once a certain degree of insight has been reached," said Wylie, " all men talk, when talk they must, the same tripe."

" Should you happen at any time," said Neary, " to feel like derogating from the general to the particular, remember I am here, and on the alert."

" My advice to you is this," said Wylie. " Leave to-night for the Great Wen——"

" What folly is this? " said Neary.

" Having first written to Miss Counihan how happy you are to be able to inform her at last that all the necessary passports and credentials to her precincts are in hand. Hers to wipe her —er—feet on. No more. No word of having gone, no note of passion. She will sit as one might say pretty——"

" One might well," said Neary.

" For a day or two and then, in great distress of mind, lay herself out to knock into you in the street. Instead of which I shall knock into her."

" What folly is this? " said Neary. " You don't know her."

" Not know her is it," said Wylie, " when there is no single aspect of her natural body with which I am not familiar."

" What do you mean? " said Neary.

" I have worshipped her from afar," said Wylie.

" How far? " said Neary.

" Yes," said Wylie pensively, " all last June, through Zeiss glasses, at a watering place." He fell into a reverie, which Neary was a big enough man to respect. " What a bust ! " he cried at length, as though galvanised by this point in his reflections. " All centre and no circumference ! "

" No doubt," said Neary, " but is it germane ? You knock into her in the street. What then ? "

" After the prescribed exchanges," said Wylie,
" she asks casually have I seen you. From that
moment she is lost."

" But if it is merely a matter of getting me out
of the way," said Neary, " while you work up
Miss Counihan, why need I go to London ? Why
not Bray ? "

The thought of going to London was distasteful
to Neary for a number of reasons, of which by
no means the least cogent was the presence there
of his second deserted wife. Strictly speaking
this woman, a née Cox, was not his wife, and
he owed her no duty, since his first deserted wife
was alive and well in Calcutta. But the lady in
London did not take this view and neither did
her legal advisers. Wylie knew something of this
position.

" To control Cooper," said Wylie, " who has
probably gone on the booze or been got at or
both."

" But would it not be possible," said Neary,
" with your priceless collaboration, to work it
from this end altogether and drop Murphy ? "

" I greatly fear," said Wylie, " that so long as
Murphy is even a remote possibility Miss Counihan will not parley. All I can do is establish
you firmly in the position of first come-down."

Neary again buried his head in his hands.

" Cathleen," said Wylie, " tell the Professor the worst."

" Eight sixes forty-eight," said Cathleen, " and twos sixteen one pound."

In the street Neary said :

" Wylie, why are you so kind ? "

" I don't seem able to control myself," said Wylie, " in the presence of certain predicaments."

" You shall find me I think not ungrateful," said Neary.

They went a little way in silence.   Then Neary said :

" I cannot think what women see in Murphy."

But Wylie was absorbed in the problem of what it was, in the predicaments of men like Neary, that carried him so far out of his government.

" Can you ? " said Neary.

Wylie considered for a moment.   Then he said :

" It is his——" stopping for want of the right word.   There seemed to be, for once, a right word.

" His what ? " said Neary.

They went a little further in silence.   Neary gave up listening for an answer and raised his face to the sky.   The gentle rain was trying not to fall.

" His surgical quality," said Wylie.

It was not quite the right word.

5

THE room that Celia had found was in Brewery
Road between Pentonville Prison and the Metro-
politan Cattle Market. West Brompton knew
them no more. The room was large and the
few articles of furniture it contained were large.
The bed, the gas cooker, the table and the
solitary tallboy, all were very large indeed. Two
massive upright unupholstered armchairs, similar
to those killed under him by Balzac, made it just
possible for them to take their meals seated.
Murphy's rocking-chair trembled by the hearth,
facing the window. The vast floor area was
covered all over by a linoleum of exquisite design,
a dim geometry of blue, grey and brown that
delighted Murphy because it called Braque to his
mind, and Celia because it delighted Murphy.
Murphy was one of the elect, who require everything to remind them of something else. The
walls were distempered a vivid lemon, Murphy's
lucky colour. This was so far in excess of the
squeeze prescribed by Suk that he could not feel

quite easy in his mind about it. The ceiling was lost in the shadows, yes, really lost in the shadows.

Here they entered upon what Celia called the new life. Murphy was inclined to think that the new life, if it came at all, came later, and then to one of them only. But Celia was so set on computing it from the hegira to the heights of Islington that he left it so. He did not want to gainsay her any more.

An immediate flaw in the new life was the landlady, a small thin worrier called Miss Carridge, a woman of such astute rectitude that she not only refused to cook the bill for Mr. Quigley, but threatened to inform that poor gentleman of how she had been tempted.

" A lady," said Murphy bitterly, " not a landlady. Thin lips and a Doric pelvis. We are P.G.s."

" All the more reason to find work," said Celia.

Everything that happened became with Celia yet another reason for Murphy's finding work. She exhibited a morbid ingenuity in this matter. From such antagonistic occasions as a new arrival at Pentonville and a fence sold out in the Market she drew the same text. The antinomies of unmarried love can seldom have appeared to better advantage.

They persuaded Murphy that his engagement at even a small salary could not fail to annihilate, for a time at least, the visible universe for his beloved. She would have to learn what it stood for all over again. And was she not rather too old for such a feat of readaptation?

He kept these forebodings to himself, and indeed tried to suppress them, so genuine was his anxiety that for him henceforward there should be no willing and no nilling but with her, or at least as little as possible. Also he knew her retort in advance : " Then there will be nothing to distract me from you." This was the kind of Joe Miller that Murphy simply could not bear to hear revived. It had never been a good joke.

Not the least remarkable of Murphy's innumerable classifications of experience was that into jokes that had once been good jokes and jokes that had never been good jokes. What but an imperfect sense of humour could have made such a mess of chaos. In the beginning was the pun. And so on.

Celia was conscious of two equally important reasons for insisting as she did. The first was her desire to make a man of Murphy ! Yes, June to October, counting in the blockade she had almost five months' experience of Murphy, yet the image of him as a man of the world continued to beckon her on. The second was her aversion to resuming her own work, as would certainly be necessary if Murphy did not find a job before her savings, scraped together during the blockade, were exhausted. What she shrank from was not merely an occupation that she had always found dull (Mr. Kelly was mistaken in thinking her made for the life) but also the effect its resumption must have on her relations with Murphy.

Both these lines led to Murphy (everything led to Murphy), but so diversely, the one from a larval experience to a person of fantasy, the other from a complete experience to a person of fact, that only a woman and one so . . . intact as Celia could have given them equal value.

Most of the time that he was out she spent sitting in the rocking-chair with her face to the light. There was not much light, the room devoured it, but she kept her face turned to what there was. The small single window condensed its changes, as half-closed eyes see the finer values of tones, so that it was never quiet in the room, but brightening and darkening in a slow ample flicker that went on all day, brightening against the darkening that was its end. A peristalsis of light, worming its way into the dark.

She preferred sitting in the chair, steeping herself in these faint eddies till they made an amnion about her own disquiet, to walking the streets (she could not disguise her gait) or wandering in the Market, where the frenzied justification of life as an end to means threw light on Murphy's prediction, that livelihood would destroy one or two or all three of his life's goods. This view, which she had always felt absurd and wished to go on feeling so, lost something of its absurdity when she collated Murphy and the Caledonian Market.

Thus in spite of herself she began to understand as soon as he gave up trying to explain. She could not go where livings were being made without feeling that they were being made away. She could not sit for long in the chair without the impulse stirring, tremulously, as for an exquisite depravity, to be naked and bound. She tried to think of Mr. Kelly or the irrevocable days or the unattainable days, but always the moment came when no effort of thought could prevail against the sensation of being imbedded in a jelly of light, or calm the trembling of her body to be made fast.

Miss Carridge's day had a nucleus, the nice strong cup of tea that she took in the afternoon. It sometimes happened that she sat down to this elixir with the conviction of having left undone none of those things that paid and done none of those things that did not pay. Then she would pour out a cup for Celia and tiptoe with it up the stairs. Miss Carridge's method of entering a private apartment was to knock timidly on the door on the outside some time after she had closed it behind her on the inside. Not even a nice hot cup of tea in her hand could make her subject to the usual conditions of time and space in this matter. It was as though she had an accomplice.

"I have brought you——" she said.

"Come in," said Celia.

"A nice hot cup of tea," said Miss Carridge. "Drink it before it coagulates."

Now Miss Carridge smelt, with a smell that not even her nearest and dearest had ever got used to. She stood there, smelling, ravished in contemplation of her tea being taken. The irony of it was, that while Miss Carridge held her breath quite unnecessarily at the sight of Celia taking the tea, Celia could not hold hers at the smell of Miss Carridge standing over her.

"I hope you like the aroma," said Miss Carridge. "Choicest Lapsang Souchong."

She moved away with the empty cup and Celia snatched a gulp of fragrance from her own bosom. This proved to be indeed a happy inspiration, for Miss Carridge paused on the way to the door.

" Hark," she said, pointing upward.

A soft padding to and fro was audible.

" The old boy," said Miss Carridge. " Never still."

Happily Miss Carridge was a woman of few words. When body odour and volubility meet, then there is no remedy.

The old boy was believed to be a retired butler. He never left his room, except of course when absolutely obliged to, nor allowed anyone to enter it. He took in the tray that Miss Carridge left twice daily at his door, and put it out when he had eaten. Miss Carridge's " Never still " was an exaggeration, but it was true that he did spend a great deal of his time ranging his room in every direction.

It was not often that Miss Carridge so far forgot herself in the glow of domestic economy as to give away a cup of Lapsang Souchong. Most days the long trance in the chair continued unbroken until it was time to prepare a meal against Murphy's return.

The punctuality with which Murphy returned was astonishing. Literally he did not vary in this by more than a few seconds from day to day. Celia wondered how anyone so vague about time in every other way could achieve such inhuman regularity in this one instance. He explained it, when she asked him, as the product of love, which forbade him to stay away from her a moment longer than was compatible with duty, and anxiety to cultivate the sense of time as money which he had heard was highly prized in business circles.

The truth was that Murphy began to return in such good time that he arrived in Brewery Road with hours to spare. From the practical point of view he could see no difference between hanging about in Brewery Road and hanging about say in Lombard Street. His prospects of employment were the same in both places, in all places. But from the sentimental point of view the difference was most marked. Brewery Road was her forecourt, in certain moods almost her ruelle.

Murphy on the jobpath was a striking figure. Word went round among the members of the Blake League that the Master's conception of Bildad the Shuhite had come to life and was stalking about London in a green suit, seeking whom he might comfort.

But what is Bildad but a fragment of Job, as Zophar and the others are fragments of Job. The only thing Murphy was seeking was what he had not ceased to seek from the moment of his being strangled into a state of respiration—the best of himself. The Blake League was utterly mistaken in supposing him on the *qui vive* for someone wretched enough to be consoled by such maieutic saws as " How can he be clean that is born." Utterly mistaken. Murphy required for his pity no other butt than himself.

His troubles had begun early. To go back no further than the vagitus, it had not been the proper A of international concert pitch, with 435 double vibrations per second, but the double flat of this. How he winced, the honest obstetrician, a devout member of the old Dublin Orchestral Society and an amateur flautist of some merit. With what sorrow he recorded that of all the millions of little larynges cursing in unison at that particular moment, the infant Murphy's alone was off the note. To go back no further than the vagitus.

His rattle will make amends.

His suit was not green, but æruginous. This also cannot be emphasised too strongly against the Blake League. In some places it was actually as black as the day it was bought, in others a strong light was needed to bring out the livid gloss, the rest was admittedly æruginous. One beheld in fact a relic of those sanguine days

when as a theological student he had used to lie
awake night after night with Bishop Bouvier's
Supplementum ad Tractatum de Matrimonio under
his pillow. What a work that was to be sure !
A Ciné Bleu scenario in goatish Latin. Or
pondering Christ's parthian shaft : *It is finished*.

No less than the colour the cut was striking.
The jacket, a tube in its own right, descended
clear of the body as far as mid-thigh, where the
skirts were slightly reflexed like the mouth of a
bell in a mute appeal to be lifted that some found
hard to resist. The trousers in their heyday had
exhibited the same proud and inflexible autonomy
of hang. But now, broken by miles of bitter
stair till they were obliged to cling here and there
for support to the legs within, a corkscrew effect
betrayed their fatigue.

Murphy never wore a waistcoat. It made
him feel like a woman.

With regard to the material of this suit, the
bold claim was advanced by the makers that it
was holeproof. This was true in the sense that
it was entirely non-porous. It admitted no air
from the outer world, it allowed none of Murphy's
own vapours to escape. To the touch it felt like
felt rather than cloth, much size must have
entered into its composition.

These remains of a decent outfit Murphy lit

up with a perfectly plain lemon made-up bow tie presented as though in derision by a collar and dicky combination carved from a single sheet of celluloid and without seam, of a period with the suit and the last of its kind.

Murphy never wore a hat, the memories it awoke of the caul were too poignant, especially when he had to take it off.

Regress in these togs was slow and Murphy was well advised to abandon hope for the day shortly after lunch and set off on the long climb home. By far the best part of the way was the toil from King's Cross up Caledonian Road, reminding him of the toil from St. Lazare up Rue d'Amsterdam. And while Brewery Road was by no means a Boulevard de Clichy nor even des Batignolles, still it was better at the end of the hill than either of those, as asylum (after a point) is better than exile.

At the top there was the little shelter like a head on the pimple of Market Road Gardens opposite the Tripe Factory. Here Murphy loved to sit ensconced between the perfume of disinfectants from Milton House immediately to the south and the stench of stalled cattle from the corral immediately to the west. The tripe did not smell.

But now it was winter-time again, night's young

thoughts had been put back an hour, the *multis latebra opportuna* of Market Road Gardens were closed before Murphy was due back with Celia. Then he would put in the time walking round and round Pentonville Prison. Even so at evening he had walked round and round cathedrals that it was too late to enter.

He took up his stand in good time in the mouth of Brewery Road, so that when the clock in the prison tower marked six-forty-five he could get off the mark without delay. Then slowly past the last bourns, the Perseverance and Temperance Yards, the Vis Vitæ Bread Co., the Marx Cork Bath Mat Manufactory, till he stood with his key in the door waiting for the clock in the market tower to chime.

The first thing Celia must do was help him out of the suit and smile when he said " Imagine Miss Carridge in a gown of this " ; then make what she could of his face as he crouched over the fire trying to get warm, and refrain from questions ; then feed him. Then, till it was time to push him out in the morning, serenade, nocturne and albada. Yes, June to October, leaving out the blockade, their nights were still that : serenade, nocturne and albada.

Suk's theme of Murphy's heaven went everywhere with that poorly starred native. He had committed it to memory, he chanted it privately as he went along. Many times he had taken it out to destroy it, lest he fell into the hands of the enemy. But his memory was so treacherous that he did not dare. He observed its precepts to the best of his ability. The dash of lemon was not absent from his apparel. He remained constantly on his guard against the various threats to his Hyleg and whole person generally. He suffered much with his feet, and his neck was not altogether free of pain. This filled him with satisfaction. It confirmed the diagram and reduced by just so much the danger of Bright's disease, Grave's disease, strangury and fits.

But there remained certain provisions that he could not implement. He had not the right gem to ensure success, indeed he had no gem of any kind. He trembled at the thought of how this want lengthened the odds against him. The lucky number did not coincide with a Sunday for a full year to come, not until Sunday, October 4th, 1936, could the maximum chance of success attend any new venture of Murphy's. This also was a perpetual worry, as he felt sure that long before then his own little prophecy, based on the one system outside that of the heavenly bodies in which he had the least confidence, his own, would have been fulfilled.

In the matter of a career Murphy could not help feeling that his stars had been guilty of some redundance, and that once go-between had been ordained further specification was superfluous. For what was all working for a living but a procuring and a pimping for the money-bags, one's lecherous tyrants the money-bags, so that they might breed.

There seems to be a certain disharmony between the only two canons in which Murphy can feel the least confidence. So much the worse for him, no doubt.

Celia said that if he did not find work at once she would have to go back to hers. Murphy knew what that meant. No more music.

This phrase is chosen with care, lest the filthy censors should lack an occasion to commit their filthy synecdoche.

Goaded by the thought of losing Celia even were it only by night (for she had promised not to " leave " him any more), Murphy applied at a chandlery in Gray's Inn Road for the position of smart boy, fingering his lemon bow nervously. This was the first time he had actually presented himself as candidate for a definite post. Up till then he had been content to expose himself

vaguely in aloof able-bodied postures on the
fringes of the better-attended slave-markets, or
to drag from pillar to post among the agencies,
a dog's life without a dog's prerogative.

The chandlers all came galloping out to see
the smart boy.

" 'E ain't smart," said the chandler, " not by a
long chork 'e ain't."

" Nor 'e ain't a boy," said the chandler's semi-
private convenience, " not to my mind 'e ain't."

" 'E don't look rightly human to me," said the
chandlers' eldest waste product, " not rightly."

Murphy was too familiar with this attitude of
derision tinged with loathing to make the further
blunder of trying to abate it.   Sometimes it was
expressed more urbanely, sometimes less.   Its forms
were as various as the grades of the chandler
mentality, its content was one : " Thou surd ! "

He looked for somewhere to sit down.   There
was nowhere.   There had once been a small
public garden south of the Royal Free Hospital,
but now part of it lay buried under one of those
malignant proliferations of urban tissue known
as service flats and the rest was reserved for the
bacteria.

At this moment Murphy would willingly have
waived his expectation of Antepurgatory for five
minutes in his chair, renounced the lee of

Belacqua's rock and his embryonal repose, looking down at dawn across the reeds to the trembling of the austral sea and the sun obliquing to
the north as it rose, immune from expiation until
he should have dreamed it all through again,
with the downright dreaming of an infant, from
the spermarium to the crematorium.   He thought
so highly of this post-mortem situation, its advantages were present in such detail to his mind, that
he actually hoped he might live to be old.   Then
he would have a long time lying there dreaming,
watching the dayspring run through its zodiac,
before the toil up hill to Paradise.   The gradient
was outrageous, one in less than one.   God grant
no godly chandler would shorten his time with a
good prayer.

This was his Belacqua fantasy and perhaps the
most highly systematised of the whole collection.
It belonged to those that lay just beyond the
frontiers of suffering, it was the first landscape of
freedom.

He leaned weakly against the railings of the
Royal Free Hospital, multiplying his vows to
erase this vision of Zion's antipodes for ever from
his repertory if only he were immediately wafted
to his rocking-chair and allowed to rock for five
minutes.   To sit down was no longer enough, he
must insist now on lying down.   Any old clod

of the well-known English turf would do, on which he might lie down, cease to take notice and enter the landscapes where there were no chandlers and no exclusive residential cancers, but only himself improved out of all knowledge.

The nearest place he could think of was Lincoln's Inn Fields. The atmosphere there was foul, a miasma of laws. Those of the cozeners, crossbiting and conycatching and sacking and figging ; and those of the cozened, pillory and gallows. But there was grass and there were plane trees.

After a few steps in the direction of this lap that was better than none, Murphy leaned again against the railings. It was clear that he had as much chance of walking to Lincoln's Inn Fields in his present condition as he had of walking to the Cockpit, and very much less incentive. He must sit down before he could lie down. Walk before you run, sit down before you lie down. He thought for a second of splashing the fourpence he allowed himself to be allowed for his lunch on a conveyance back to Brewery Road. But then Celia would think he was quitting on the strength of her promise not to leave him, even though she had to return to her work. The only solution was to take his lunch at once, more than an hour before he was due to salivate.

Murphy's fourpenny lunch was a ritual vitiated by no base thoughts of nutrition. He advanced along the railings by easy stages until he came to a branch of the caterers he wanted. The sensation of the seat of a chair coming together with his drooping posteriors at last was so delicious that he rose at once and repeated the sit, lingeringly and with intense concentration. Murphy did not so often meet with these tendernesses that he could afford to treat them casually. The second sit, however, was a great disappointment.

The waitress stood before, with an air of such abstraction that he did not feel entitled to regard himself as an element in her situation. At last, seeing that she did not move, he said :

" Bring me," in the voice of an usher resolved to order the chef's special selection for a school outing. He paused after this preparatory signal to let the fore-period develop, that first of the three moments of reaction in which, according to the Külpe school, the major torments of response are undergone. Then he applied the stimulus proper.

" A cup of tea and a packet of assorted biscuits." Twopence the tea, twopence the biscuits, a perfectly balanced meal.

As though suddenly aware of the great magical ability, or it might have been the surgical quality, the waitress murmured, before the eddies of the main-period drifted her away : " Vera to you, dear." This was not a caress.

Murphy had some faith in the Külpe school. Marbe and Bühler might be deceived, even Watt was only human, but how could Ach be wrong ?

Vera concluded, as she thought, her performance in much better style than she had begun. It was hard to believe, as she set down the tray, that it was the same slavey. She actually made out the bill there and then on her own initiative.

Murphy pushed the tray away, tilted back his chair and considered his lunch with reverence and satisfaction. With reverence, because as an adherent (on and off) of the extreme theophanism of William of Champeaux he could not but feel humble before such sacrifices to his small but implacable appetite, nor omit the silent grace : On this part of himself that I am about to indigest may the Lord have mercy. With satisfaction, because the supreme moment in his degradations had come, the moment when, unaided and alone, he defrauded a vested interest. The sum involved was small, something between a penny and twopence (on the retail valuation). But then he had only fourpence worth of confidence to play with. His attitude simply was, that if a swindle of from twenty-five to fifty per cent of the outlay, and effected while you wait, was not a case of the large returns and quick turnover indicated by Suk, then there was a serious flaw somewhere in his theory of sharp practice. But no matter how the transaction were judged from the economic point of view, nothing could detract from its merit as a little triumph of tactics in the face of the most fearful odds. Only compare the belligerents. On the one hand a colossal league of plutomanic caterers, highly endowed with the ruthless cunning of the sane, having at their disposal all the most deadly weapons of the post-war recovery; on the other, a seedy solipsist and fourpence.

The seedy solipsist then, having said his silent grace and savoured his infamy in advance, drew up his chair briskly to the table, seized the cup of tea and half emptied it at one gulp. No sooner had this gone to the right place than he began to splutter, eructate and complain, as though he had been duped into swallowing a saturated solution of powdered glass. In this way he attracted to himself the attention not only of every customer in the saloon but actually of the waitress Vera, who came running to get a good view of the accident, as she supposed. Murphy continued for a little to make sounds as of a flushing-box taxed beyond its powers and then said, in an egg and scorpion voice :

" I ask for China and you give me Indian."

Though disappointed that it was nothing more interesting, Vera made no bones about making good her mistake. She was a willing little bit of sweated labour, incapable of betraying the slogan of her slavers, that since the customer or sucker was paying for his gutrot ten times what it cost to produce and five times what it cost to fling in his face, it was only reasonable to defer to his complaints up to but not exceeding fifty per cent of his exploitation.

With the fresh cup of tea Murphy adopted quite a new technique. He drank not more than a third of it and then waited till Vera happened to be passing.

" I am most fearfully sorry," he said, " Vera, to give you all this trouble, but do you think it would be possible to have this filled with hot ? "

Vera showing signs of bridling, Murphy uttered winningly the sesame.

" I know I am a great nuisance, but they have been too generous with the cowjuice."

Generous and cowjuice were the keywords here. No waitress could hold out against their mingled overtones of gratitude and mammary organs. And Vera was essentially a waitress.

That is the end of how Murphy defrauded a vested interest every day for his lunch, to the honourable extent of paying for one cup of tea and consuming 1·8⅓ cups approximately.

Try it sometime, gentle skimmer.

He was now feeling so much better that he conceived the bold project of reserving the biscuits for later in the afternoon. He would finish the tea, then have as much free milk and sugar as he could lay his hands on, then walk carefully to the Cockpit and there eat the biscuits. Someone in Oxford Street might offer him a position of the highest trust. He settled down to plan how exactly he would get from where he was to Tottenham Court Road, what cutting reply he would make to the magnate and in what order he would eat the biscuits when the time came. He had proceeded no further than the British Museum and was recruiting himself in the Archaic Room before the Harpy Tomb, when a sharp surface thrust against his nose caused him to open his eyes. This proved to be a visiting-card which was at once withdrawn so that he might read :

Austin Ticklepenny
Pot Poet
From the County of Dublin

This creature does not merit any particular

description. The merest pawn in the game between Murphy and his stars, he makes his little move, engages an issue and is swept from the board. Further use may conceivably be found for Austin Ticklepenny in a child's halma or a book-reviewer's snakes and ladders, but his chess days are over. There is no return game between a man and his stars.

"When I failed to gain your attention," said Ticklepenny, "by means of what the divine son of Ariston calls the vocal stream issuing from the soul through the lips, I took the liberty as you notice."

Murphy drained his cup and made to rise. But Ticklepenny trapped his legs under the table and said :

"Fear not, I have ceased to sing."

Murphy had such an enormous contempt for rape that he found it no trouble to go quite limp at the first sign of its application. He did so now.

"Yes," said Ticklepenny, "*nulla linea sine die*. Would I be here if I were not on the water-tumbril ? I would not."

He worked up to such a pitch his gambadoes under the table that Murphy's memory began to vibrate.

"Didn't I have the dishonour once in Dublin," he said. " Can it have been at the Gate ? "

" *Romiet*," said Ticklepenny, " *and Juleo*. ' Take him and cut him out in little stars . . .' Wotanope ! "

Murphy dimly remembered an opportune apothecary.

" I was snout drunk," said Ticklepenny. " You were dead drunk."

Now the sad truth was that Murphy never touched it. This was bound to come out sooner or later.

" Unless you want me to call a policewoman," said Murphy, " cease your clumsy genustuprations."

Woman was the keyword here.

" My liver dried up," said Ticklepenny, " so I had to hang up my lyre."

" And let yourself go fundamentally," said Murphy.

" Messrs. Melpomene, Calliope, Erato and Thalia," said Ticklepenny, " in that order, woo me in vain since my change of life."

" Then you know how I feel," said Murphy.

" That same Ticklepenny," said Ticklepenny, " who for more years than he cares to remember turned out his steady pentameter per pint, day in, day out, is now degraded to the position of male nurse in a hospital for the better-class mentally deranged. It is the same Ticklepenny, but God bless my soul *quantum mutatus*."

" *Ab illa*," said Murphy.

" I sit on them that will not eat," said Ticklepenny, " jacking their jaws apart with the gag, spurning their tongues aside with the spatula, till the last tundish of drench is absorbed. I go round the cells with my shovel and bucket, I——"

Ticklepenny broke down, took indeed a large draught of his lemon phosphate, and altogether ceased his wooing under the table. Murphy could not take advantage of this to go, being stunned by the sudden clash between two hitherto distinct motifs in Suk's delineations, that of lunatic in paragraph two and that of custodian in paragraph seven.

" I cannot stand it," groaned Ticklepenny, " it is driving me mad."

It is hard to say where the fault lies in the case of Ticklepenny, whether with the soul, the stream or the lips, but certainly the quality of his speech is most wretched. Celia's confidence to Mr. Kelly, Neary's to Wylie, had to be given for the most part obliquely. With all the more reason now, Ticklepenny's to Murphy. It will not take many moments.

After much hesitation Ticklepenny consulted

a Dublin physician, a Dr. Fist more philosophical than medical, German on his father's side. Dr. Fist said : " Giff de pooze ub or go kaputt." Ticklepenny said he would give up the booze. Dr. Fist laughed copiously and said : " I giff yous a shit to Killiecrrrankie." Dr. Angus Killiecrankie was R.M.S. to an institution on the outskirts of London known as the Magdalen Mental Mercyseat. The chit proposed that Ticklepenny, a distinguished indigent drunken Irish bard, should make himself useful about the place in return for a mild course of dipso-pathic discipline.

Ticklepenny responded so rapidly to this arrangement that the rumour of a misdiagnosis began to raise its horrid head in the M.M.M., until Dr. Fist wrote from Dublin explaining that the curative factor at work in this interesting case was to be sought neither in the dipsopathy nor in the bottlewashing, but in the freedom from poetic composition that these conferred on his client, whose breakdown had been due less to the pints than to the pentameters.

This view of the matter will not seem strange to anyone familiar with the class of pentameter that Ticklepenny felt it his duty to Erin to compose, as free as a canary in the fifth foot (a cruel sacrifice, for Ticklepenny hiccuped in end rimes) and at the cæsura as hard and fast as his own divine flatus and otherwise bulging with as many minor beauties from the gaelic prosodoturfy as could be sucked out of a mug of Beamish's porter. No wonder he felt a new man washing the bottles and emptying the slops of the better-class mentally deranged.

But all good things come to an end and Ticklepenny was offered a job in the wards at the seneschalesque figure of five pounds a month all found. He accepted. He no longer had the spirit to refuse. The Olympian sot had reverted to the temperate potboy.

Now after a bare week in the wards he felt he could not go on. He did not mind having his pity and even his terror titillated within reason, but the longing to vomit with compassion and anxiety struck him as repugnant to the true catharsis, especially as he could never bring anything up.

Ticklepenny was immeasurably inferior to Neary in every way, but they had certain points of contrast with Murphy in common. One was this pretentious fear of going mad. Another was the inability to look on, no matter what the spectacle. These were connected, in the sense that the painful situation could always be reduced to onlooking of one kind or another.

But even here Neary was superior to Ticklepenny, at least according to the tradition that
ranks the competitor's spirit higher than the
huckster's and the man regretting what he cannot have higher than the man sneering at what
he cannot understand. For Neary knew his
great master's figure of the three lives, whereas
Ticklepenny knew nothing.

Wylie came a little closer to Murphy, but his
way of looking was as different from Murphy's
as a *voyeur's* from a *voyant's*, though Wylie was
no more the one in the indecent sense than
Murphy was the other in the supradecent sense.
The terms are only taken to distinguish between
the vision that depends on light, object, view-
point, etc., and the vision that all those things
embarrass. In the days when Murphy was
concerned with seeing Miss Counihan, he had
had to close his eyes to do so. And even now
when he closed them there was no guarantee
that Miss Counihan would not appear. That
was Murphy's really yellow spot. Similarly he
had seen Celia for the first time, not when she
revolved before him in the way that so delighted
Mr. Kelly, but while she was away consulting
the Reach. It was as though some instinct had
withheld her from accosting him in form until
he should have obtained a clear view of her

advantages, and warned her that before he could see it had to be not merely dark, but his own dark. Murphy believed there was no dark quite like his own dark.

Ticklepenny's pompous dread of being driven mad by the spectacle constantly before him of those that were so already, made him long most heartily to throw up his job as male nurse at the Magdalen Mental Mercyseat. But as he had been admitted on probation for the term of one month, nothing less than a month's service would produce any pay. To throw up the job at the end of a week or a fortnight or any period less than the period of probation would mean no compensation for all he had suffered. And between going mad and having the rest of his life poisoned by the thought of having once worked for a week for nothing, Ticklepenny found little to choose.

Even the M.M.M. found it no easier than other mental hospitals to procure nurses. This was one reason for the enlistment of Ticklepenny, whose only qualifications for handling the mentally deranged were the pot poet's bulk and induration to abuse. For even in the M.M.M. there were not many patients so divorced from reality that they could not discern and vituperate a Ticklepenny in their midst.

When Ticklepenny had quite done com-
miserating himself, in a snivelling antiphony
between the cruel necessity of going mad if he
stayed and the cruel impossibility of leaving
without his wages, Murphy said :

" Supposing you were to produce a substitute
of my intelligence " (corrugating his brow) " and
physique " (squaring the circle of his shoulders),
" what then ? "

These words sent the whole of Ticklepenny
into transports, but no part of him so horribly
as his knees, which began to fawn under the
table. Even so a delighted dog will sometimes
forget himself.

When this had exhausted itself he begged
Murphy to accompany him without a moment's
delay to the M.M.M. and be signed on, as though
the possibility of opposition on the part of the
authorities to this lightning change in their
personnel were too remote to be considered.
Murphy also was inclined to think that the
arrangement would find immediate favour,
assuming that Ticklepenny had concealed no
material factor in the situation, such as a liaison
with some high official, the head male nurse
for example. Short of being such a person's
minion, Murphy was inclined to think there
was nothing Ticklepenny could do that he could

not do a great deal better, especially in a society of psychotics, and that they had merely to appear together before the proper authority for this to be patent.

But what made Murphy feel really confident was the sudden syzygy in Suk's delineations of lunatic in paragraph two and custodian in paragraph seven. Of these considered separately up to date the first had seemed a mere monthly prognosticator's tag, compelled by the presence of the moon in the Serpent, and the second a truism on the part of his stars. Now their union made the nativity appear as finely correlated in all its parts as the system from which it purported to come.

Thus this sixpence worth of sky, from the ludicrous broadsheet that Murphy had called his life-warrant, his bull of incommunication and corpus of deterrents, changed into the poem that he alone of the living could write. He drew out the black envelope, grasped it to tear it across, then put it back in his pocket, mindful of his memory, and that he was not alone. He said he would present himself at the M.M.M. the following Sunday morning, whenever that was, which would give Tickle-penny time to manure the ground. Tickle-penny would not go mad before that day of rest so favourable to Murphy. To those in fear of losing it, reason stuck like a bur. And to those in hope . . . ?

" Call me Austin," said Ticklepenny, " or even Augustin." He felt the time was hardly ripe for Gussy, or even Gus.

Having now been seated for over an hour without any ill effects, carried through his daily fraud and found a use for a pot poet, Murphy felt he had earned the long rapture flat on his back in that most pleasant of natural laps available, the Cockpit in Hyde Park. The need for this had been steadily increasing, now in a final spasm of urgency it tore him away from Ticklepenny, into the Gray's Inn Road. Under the table the legs continued to fawn, as a fowl to writhe long after its head has been removed, on a void place and a spacious nothing.

Vera, remarking that he did not call at the cash-desk on his way out and that his bill lay where she had put it, supposed the onus of payment to have fallen on the friend. However she made quite sure that it would not fall on her by putting the two bills together when she made out the second. All this happened as Murphy had foreseen. The comfort he had been to Ticklepenny was dirt cheap at fourpence.

Half the filth thus saved went on a bus to

the Marble Arch. He told the conductor to tell him when they got there, so that he might close his eyes and keep them closed. This cancelled the magnate in Oxford Street, but what were magnates to a man whose future was assured? And as for the Harpy Tomb, by closing his eyes he could be in an archaic world very much less corrupt than anything on view in the B.M. Crawling and jerking along in the bus he tried to think of Celia's face when she heard of the engagement, he even tried to think of the engagement itself, but his skull felt packed with gelatine and he could not think of anything.

Murphy adored many things, to think of him as sad or blasé would be to do him an injustice or too much honour. One of the many things that he adored was a ride in one of the new six-wheelers when the traffic was at its height. The deep oversprung seats were most insidious, especially forward. A staple recreation before Celia had been to wait at Walham Green for a nice number eleven and take it through the evening rush to Liverpool Street and back, sitting downstairs behind the driver on the near side. But now with Celia to support, and Miss Carridge making her own of his uncle's interests, this pleasure lay beyond his means.

Near the Cockpit a guffawing group was watching Rima being cleaned of a copious pollution of red permanganate. Murphy receded a little way into the north and prepared to finish his lunch. He took the biscuits carefully out of the packet and laid them face upward on the grass, in order as he felt of edibility. They were the same as always, a Ginger, an Osborne, a Digestive, a Petit Beurre and one anonymous. He always ate the first-named last, because he liked it the best, and the anonymous first, because he thought it very likely the least palatable. The order in which he ate the remaining three was indifferent to him and varied irregularly from day to day. On his knees now before the five it struck him for the first time that these prepossessions reduced to a paltry six the number of ways in which he could make this meal. But this was to violate the very essence of assortment, this was red permanganate on the Rima of variety. Even if he conquered his prejudice against the anonymous, still there would be only twenty-four ways in which the biscuits could be eaten. But were he to take the final step and overcome his infatuation with the ginger, then the assortment would spring to life before him, dancing the radiant measure of its total permutability, edible in a hundred and twenty ways !

Overcome by these perspectives Murphy fell forward on his face on the grass, beside those biscuits of which it could be said as truly as of the stars, that one differed from another, but of which he could not partake in their fullness until he had learnt not to prefer any one to any other. Lying beside them on the grass but facing the opposite way, wrestling with the demon of gingerbread, he heard the words :

" Would you have the goodness, pardon the intrusion, to hold my little doggy? "

Seen from above and behind Murphy did look fairly obliging, the kind of stranger one's little doggy would not mind being held by. He sat up and found himself at the feet of a low-sized corpulent middle-aged woman with very bad duck's disease indeed.

Duck's disease is a distressing pathological condition in which the thighs are suppressed and the buttocks spring directly from behind the knees, aptly described in Steiss's nosonomy as Panpygoptosis. Happily its incidence is small and confined, as the popular name suggests, to the weaker vessel, a bias of Nature bitterly lamented by the celebrated Dr. Busby and other less pedantic notables. It is non-contagious (though some observers have held the contrary), non-infectious, non-heritable, painless and intractable. Its ætiology remains obscure to all but the psychopathological wholehogs, who have shown it to be simply another embodiment of the neurotic *Non me rebus sed mihi res*.

The Duck, to give her a name to go on with, held in one hand a large bulging bag and in the other a lead whereby her personality was extended to a Dachshund so low and so long that Murphy had no means of telling whether it was a dog or a bitch, which was the first thing he always wanted to know about every so-called dog that came before him. It certainly had the classical bitch's eye, kiss me in the cornea, keep me in the iris and God help you in the pupil. But some dogs had that.

Murphy's front did not bear out the promise of his rear, but the Duck had gone too far to draw back.

"Nelly is in heat," she said, without the least trace of affectation, in a voice both proud and sad, and paused for Murphy to congratulate or condole, according to his lights. When he did neither she simply laid down her hand.

"The oui-ja board is how I live, I come all

the way from Paddington to feed the poor dear
sheep and now I dare not let her off, here is
my card, Rosie Dew, single woman, by appointment to Lord Gall of Wormwood, perhaps you
know him, a charming man, he sends me objects,
he is in a painful position, spado of long standing
in tail male special he seeks testamentary penti-
menti from the *au-delà*, how she strains to be
off and away, the protector is a man of iron
and will not bar, plunge the fever of her blood
in the Serpentine or the Long Water for that
matter, like Shelley's first wife you know, her
name was Harriet was it not, not Nelly, Shelley,
Nelly, oh Nelly how I ADORE you."

Shortening her hold on the lead she whipped
up Nelly with great dexterity into the wilds
of her bosom and covered her snout with all
the kisses that Nelly had taught her in the long
evenings.   She then handed the trembling animal
to Murphy, took two heads of lettuce out of the
bag and began sidling up to the sheep.

The sheep were a miserable-looking lot, dingy,
close-cropped, undersized and misshapen.   They
were not cropping, they were not ruminating,
they did not even seem to be taking their ease.
They simply stood, in an attitude of profound
dejection, their heads bowed, swaying slightly
as though dazed. Murphy had never seen

stranger sheep, they seemed one and all on the point of collapse. They made the exposition of Wordsworth's lovely " fields of sleep " as a compositor's error for " fields of sheep " seem no longer a jibe at that most excellent man. They had not the strength to back away from Miss Dew approaching with the lettuce.

She moved freely among them, tendering the lettuce to one after another, pressing it up into their sunk snouts with the gesture of one feeding sugar to a horse. They turned their broody heads aside from the emetic, bringing them back into alignment as soon as it passed from them. Miss Dew strayed further and further afield in her quest for a sheep to eat her lettuce.

Murphy had been too absorbed in this touching little argonautic, and above all in the ecstatic demeanour of the sheep, to pay any attention to Nelly. He now discovered that she had eaten all the biscuits with the exception of the Ginger, which cannot have remained in her mouth for more than a couple of seconds. She was seated after her meal, to judge by the infinitesimal angle that her back was now making with the horizon. There is this to be said for Dachshunds of such length and lowness as Nelly, that it makes very little difference to

their appearance whether they stand, sit or lie.
If Parmigianino had gone in for painting dogs,
he would have painted them like Nelly.

Miss Dew was now experimenting with quite
a new technique. This consisted in placing her
offering on the ground and withdrawing to a
discreet remove, so that the sheep might separate
in their minds, if that was what they wanted,
the ideas of the giver and the gift. Miss Dew
was not Love, that she could feel one with what
she gave, and perhaps there was some dark
ovine awareness of this, that Miss Dew was
not lettuce, holding up the entire works. But
a sheep's psychology is far less simple than
Miss Dew had any idea, and the lettuce mas-
querading as a natural product of the park met
with no more success than when presented
frankly as an exotic variety.

Miss Dew at last was obliged to admit defeat,
a bitter pill to have to swallow before a perfect
stranger. She picked up the two heads of lettuce
and came trundling back on her powerful little
legs to where Murphy was sitting on his heels,
bemoaning his loss. She stood beside him too
abashed to speak, whereas he was too aggrieved
not to.

" The sheep," he said, " may not fancy your
cabbage——"

" Lettuce ! " cried Miss Dew. " Lovely fresh clean white crisp sparkling delicious lettuce ! "

" But your hot dog has eaten my lunch," said Murphy, " or as much of it as she could stomach."

Miss Dew went down on her knees just like any ordinary person and took Nelly's head in her hands. Mistress and bitch exchanged a long look of intelligence.

" The depravity of her appetite," said Murphy, " you may be glad to hear, does not extend to ginger, nor the extremity of mine to a rutting cur's rejectamenta."

Miss Dew kneeling looked more than ever like a duck, or a stunted penguin. Her bosom rose and fell, her colour came and went, in consequence of Murphy's reference to Nelly, who with Lord Gall was almost all she had in this dreary *en-deçà*, as a rutting cur. Her pet had certainly placed her in a very false position.

Wylie in Murphy's place might have consoled himself with the thought that the Park was a closed system in which there could be no loss of appetite ; Neary with the unction of an *Ipse dixit* ; Ticklepenny with reprisal. But Murphy was inconsolable, the snuff of the dip stinking that the biscuits had lit in his mind, for Nelly to extinguish.

" Oh, my America," he cried, " my Newfound-
land, no sooner sighted than Atlantis."

Miss Dew pictured her patron in her place.
" How much are you out ? " she said.

These words were incomprehensible to Murphy,
and remained so until he saw a purse in her
hand.

" Twopence," he replied, " and a critique of
pure love."

" Here is threepence," said Miss Dew.

This brought Murphy's filth up to fivepence.

Miss Dew went away without saying good-
bye. She had not left home more gladly than she
now returned sadly. It was often the way. She
trundled along towards Victoria Gate, Nelly
gliding before her, and felt the worse for her
outing. Her lettuce turned down, her mortification, her pet and herself in her pet insulted,
the threepence gone that she had earmarked
for a glass of mild. She passed by the dahlias
and the dogs' cemetery, out into the sudden
grey glare of Bayswater Road. She caught up
Nelly in her arms and carried her a greater
part of the way to Paddington than was necessary.
A boot was waiting for her from Lord Gall,
a boot formerly in the wardrobe of his father.
She would sit down with Nelly in her lap, one
hand on the boot, the other on the board, and

wrest from the ether some good reason for the protector, who was also the reversioner unfortunately, to cut off the cruel entail.

Miss Dew's control, a panpygoptotic Manichee of the fourth century, Lena by name, severe of deportment and pallid of feature, who had entertained Jerome on his way through Rome from Calchis to Bethlehem, had not, according to her own account, been raised so wholly a spiritual body as yet to sit down with much more comfort than she had in the natural. But she declared that every century brought a marked improvement and urged Miss Dew to be of good courage. In a thousand years she might look forward to having thighs like anyone else, and not merely thighs, but thighs celestial.

Miss Dew was no ordinary hack medium, her methods were original and eclectic. She might not be able to bring down torrents of ectoplasm or multiply anemones from her armpits, but left undisturbed with one hand on a disaffected boot, the other on the board, Nelly in her lap and Lena coming through, she could make the dead softsoap the quick in seven languages.

Murphy continued to sit on his heels for some little time, playing with the five pennies, speculating on Miss Dew, speculating on the sheep with whom he felt in close sympathy, deprecating this prejudice and that, arraigning his love of Celia. In vain. The freedom of indifference, the indifference of freedom, the will dust in the dust of its object, the act a handful of sand let fall—these were some of the shapes he had sighted, sunset landfall after many days. But now all was nebulous and dark, a murk of irritation from which no spark could be excogitated. He therefore went to the other extreme, disconnected his mind from the gross importunities of sensation and reflection and composed himself on the hollow of his back for the torpor he had been craving to enter for the past five hours. He had been unavoidably detained, by Ticklepenny, by Miss Dew, by his efforts to rekindle the light that Nelly had quenched. But now there seemed nothing to stop him. Nothing can stop me now, was his last thought before he lapsed into consciousness, and nothing will stop me. In effect, nothing did turn up to stop him and he slipped away, from the pensums and prizes, from Celia, chandlers, public highways, etc., from Celia, buses, public gardens, etc., to where there were no pensums and no prizes, but only Murphy himself, improved out of all knowledge.

When he came to, or rather from, how he had no idea, he found night fallen, a full moon risen and the sheep gathered round him, a drift of pale uneasy shapes, suggesting how he might have been roused. They seemed in rather better form, less Wordsworthy, resting, ruminating and even cropping. What they had rejected was therefore not Miss Dew, nor her cabbage, but simply the hour of day. He thought of the four caged owls in Battersea Park, whose joys and sorrows did not begin till dusk.

He bared his eyes to the moon, he forced back the lids with his fingers, the yellow oozed under them into his skull, a belch came wet and foul from the green old days—

> Gazed on unto my setting from my rise
> Almost of none but of unquiet eyes—,

he spat, rose and hastened back to Celia, with all the speed that fivepence could command. No doubt his news was good, according to her God, but it had been a trying day for Murphy in the body and he was more than usually impatient for the music to begin. It was long past his usual hour when he arrived, to find, not a meal spoiling as he had hoped and feared, but Celia spreadeagled on her face on the bed.

A shocking thing had happened.

6

Amor intellectualis quo Murphy se ipsum amat.

IT is most unfortunate, but the point of this
story has been reached where a justification
of the expression " Murphy's mind " has to
be attempted. Happily we need not concern
ourselves with this apparatus as it really was
—that would be an extravagance and an im-
pertinence—but solely with what it felt and
pictured itself to be. Murphy's mind is after
all the gravamen of these informations. A short
section to itself at this stage will relieve us from
the necessity of apologising for it further.

Murphy's mind pictured itself as a large
hollow sphere, hermetically closed to the universe
without. This was not an impoverishment, for
it excluded nothing that it did not itself contain.
Nothing ever had been, was or would be in
the universe outside it but was already present
as virtual, or actual, or virtual rising into actual,
or actual falling into virtual, in the universe
inside it.

This did not involve Murphy in the idealist tar. There was the mental fact and there was the physical fact, equally real if not equally pleasant.

He distinguished between the actual and the virtual of his mind, not as between form and the formless yearning for form, but as between that of which he had both mental and physical experience and that of which he had mental experience only. Thus the form of kick was actual, that of caress virtual.

The mind felt its actual part to be above and bright, its virtual beneath and fading into dark, without however connecting this with the ethical yoyo. The mental experience was cut off from the physical experience, its criteria were not those of the physical experience, the agreement of part of its content with physical fact did not confer worth on that part. It did not function and could not be disposed according to a principle of worth. It was made up of light fading into dark, of above and beneath, but not of good and bad. It contained forms with parallel in another mode and forms without, but not right forms and wrong forms. It felt no issue between its light and dark, no need for its light to devour its dark. The need was now to be in the light, now in the half light, now in the dark. That was all.

Thus Murphy felt himself split in two, a body and a mind. They had intercourse apparently, otherwise he could not have known that they had anything in common. But he felt his mind to be bodytight and did not understand through what channel the intercourse was effected nor how the two experiences came to overlap. He was satisfied that neither followed from the other. He neither thought a kick because he felt one nor felt a kick because he thought one. Perhaps the knowledge was related to the fact of the kick as two magnitudes to a third. Perhaps there was, outside space and time, a non-mental non-physical Kick from all eternity, dimly revealed to Murphy in its correlated modes of consciousness and extension, the kick *in intellectu* and the kick *in re*. But where then was the supreme Caress?

However that might be, Murphy was content to accept this partial congruence of the world of his mind with the world of his body as due to some such process of supernatural determination. The problem was of little interest. Any solution would do that did not clash with the feeling, growing stronger as Murphy grew older, that his mind was a closed system, subject to no principle of change but its own, self-sufficient and impermeable to the vicissitudes of the body.

Of infinitely more interest than how this came to be so was the manner in which it might be exploited.

He was split, one part of him never left this mental chamber that pictured itself as a sphere full of light fading into dark, because there was no way out. But motion in this world depended on rest in the world outside. A man is in bed, wanting to sleep. A rat is behind the wall at his head, wanting to move. The man hears the rat fidget and cannot sleep, the rat hears the man fidget and dares not move. They are both unhappy, one fidgeting and the other waiting, or both happy, the rat moving and the man sleeping.

Murphy could think and know after a fashion with his body up (so to speak) and about, with a kind of mental *tic douloureux* sufficient for his parody of rational behaviour. But that was not what he understood by consciousness.

His body lay down more and more in a less precarious abeyance than that of sleep, for its own convenience and so that the mind might move. There seemed little left of this body that was not privy to this mind, and that little was usually tired on its own account. The development of what looked like collusion between such utter strangers remained to Murphy as unintelligible as telekinesis or the Leyden Jar, and of as little interest. He noted with satisfaction that it existed, that his bodily need ran more and more with his mental.

As he lapsed in body he felt himself coming alive in mind, set free to move among its treasures. The body has its stock, the mind its treasures.

There were the three zones, light, half light, dark, each with its speciality.

In the first were the forms with parallel, a radiant abstract of the dog's life, the elements of physical experience available for a new arrangement. Here the pleasure was reprisal, the pleasure of reversing the physical experience. Here the kick that the physical Murphy received, the mental Murphy gave. It was the same kick, but corrected as to direction. Here the chandlers were available for slow depilation, Miss Carridge for rape by Ticklepenny, and so on. Here the whole physical fiasco became a howling success.

In the second were the forms without parallel. Here the pleasure was contemplation. This system had no other mode in which to be out of joint and therefore did not need to be put right in this. Here was the Belacqua bliss and others scarcely less precise.

In both these zones of his private world
Murphy felt sovereign and free, in the one to
requite himself, in the other to move as he
pleased from one unparalleled beatitude to
another. There was no rival initiative.

The third, the dark, was a flux of forms, a
perpetual coming together and falling asunder
of forms. The light contained the docile elements of a new manifold, the world of the body
broken up into the pieces of a toy; the half
light, states of peace. But the dark neither
elements nor states, nothing but forms becoming
and crumbling into the fragments of a new
becoming, without love or hate or any intel-
ligible principle of change. Here there was
nothing but commotion and the pure forms of
commotion. Here he was not free, but a mote
in the dark of absolute freedom. He did not
move, he was a point in the ceaseless un-
conditioned generation and passing away of line.

Matrix of surds.

It was pleasant to kick the Ticklepennies
and Miss Carridges simultaneously together into
ghastly acts of love. It was pleasant to lie
dreaming on the shelf beside Belacqua,
watching the dawn break crooked. But how
much more pleasant was the sensation of being
a missile without provenance or target, caught

up in a tumult of non-Newtonian motion. So pleasant that pleasant was not the word.

Thus as his body set him free more and more in his mind, he took to spending less and less time in the light, spitting at the breakers of the world ; and less in the half light, where the choice of bliss introduced an element of effort ; and more and more and more in the dark, in the will-lessness, a mote in its absolute freedom.

This painful duty having now been discharged, no further bulletins will be issued.

7

CELIA's triumph over Murphy, following her confidence to her grandfather, was gained about the middle of September, Thursday the 12th to be pedantic, a little before the Ember Days, the sun being still in the Virgin. Wylie rescued Neary, consoled and advised him, a week later, as the sun with a sigh of relief passed over into the Balance. The encounter, on which so much unhinges, between Murphy and Ticklepenny, took place on Friday, October the 11th (though Murphy did not know that), the moon being full again, but not nearly so near the earth as when last in opposition.

Let us now take Time that old fornicator, bald though he be behind, by such few sad short hairs as he has, back to Monday, October the 7th, the first day of his restitution to the bewitching Miss Greenwich.

Respectable people were going to bed.

Mr. Willoughby Kelly lay back. The sail of his kite was crimson silk, worn and wan with

much exposure. He had been mending it with
needle and thread, he could do no more, it
lay a large hexagon of crimson on the counterpane, freed from its asterisk of sticks. Mr.
Kelly himself did not look a day over ninety,
cascades of light from the bed-lamp fell on the
hairless domes and bosses of his skull, scored
his ravaged face with shadow. He found it
hard to think, his body seemed spread over a
vast area, parts would wander away and get
lost if he did not keep a sharp look-out, he felt
them fidgeting to be off. He was vigilant and
agitated, his vigilance was agitated, he made
snatches and darts in his mind at this part
and that. He found it hard to think, impossible
to expand the sad pun (for he had excellent
French) : *Celia, s'il y a, Celia, s'il y a*, throbbing
steadily behind his eyes. To be punning her
name consoled him a little, a very little. What
had he done to her, that she did not come to
see him any more ? Now I have no one, said
Mr. Kelly, not even Celia. The human eyelid
is not teartight, the craters between nose and
cheekbones trapped the precious moisture, no
other lachrymatory was necessary.

Neary also had no one, not even Cooper.
He sat in Glasshouse Street, huddled in the

tod of his troubles like an owl in ivy, inundating
with green tea a bellyful of bird's-nest soup,
chop suey, noodles, sharks' fins and ly-chee
syrup. He was sad, with the snarling sadness
of the choleric man. With the chop-sticks
held like bones between his fingers he kept up
a low battuta of anger.

His problem was not only how to find Murphy,
but how to find him without being found himself
by Ariadne née Cox. It was like looking for
a needle in a haystack full of vipers. The town
was alive with her touts, with her multitudinous
self, and he was alone. In a moment of fury
he had cast off Cooper, whom now when he
longed to have back he could not find. He
had written begging Wylie to come and support
him, with his resource, his practical ingenuity,
his *savoir faire*, his *savoir ne pas faire*, all those
vulpine endowments that Neary did not possess.
To which Wylie had replied, very truly, that
Miss Counihan was a wholetime job and the
straightening of Neary's way a harder nut to
crack than he had anticipated. This letter
filled Neary with a new misgiving. He had
been let down by Cooper, a tried and trusted
servant ; with how much more likelihood then
by Wylie, whom he scarcely knew. All of a
sudden Murphy, his quarry, seemed the only

man of all his acquaintance, of all the men he had ever known, who would not fail in his trust to a man, however badly he might seem to treat women. Thus his need for Murphy changed. It could not be more urgent than it was, it had to lose with reference to the rival what it gained with reference to the friend. The horse leech's daughter was a closed system.

He sat on, shaking his head like a perhaps empty bottle, muttering bitterly with the chopsticks, and a sorer lack than any wife or even mistress, were she Yang Kuei-fei herself, was a mind to pillow his beside. The Oriental milieu had no doubt to do with this aberration. The ly-chee, of which he had taken three portions, continued to elaborate its nameless redolence, a dusk of lute music behind his troubles.

Miss Counihan sat on Wylie's knees, *not* in Wynn's Hotel lest an action for libel should lie, and oyster kisses passed between them. Wylie did not often kiss, but when he did it was a serious matter. He was not one of those lugubrious persons who insist on removing the clapper from the bell of passion. A kiss from Wylie was like a breve tied, in a long slow amorous phrase, over bars' times its equivalent in demi-semiquavers. Miss Counihan had never enjoyed anything quite so much as this slow-motion osmosis of love's spittle.

The above passage is carefully calculated to deprave the cultivated reader.

For an Irish girl Miss Counihan was quite exceptionally anthropoid. Wylie was not sure that he cared altogether for her mouth, which was a large one. The kissing surface was greater than the rosebud's, but less highly toned. Otherwise she did. It is superfluous to describe her, she was just like any other beautiful Irish girl, except, as noted, more markedly anthropoid. How far this constitutes an advantage is what every man must decide for himself.

Enter Cooper. Like a mollusc torn from its rock Wylie came away. Miss Counihan staunched her mouth. Wylie would not have broken off his love game for Cooper, any more than for an animal, but he feared lest Neary also were at hand.

" I do be turned off," said Cooper.

Wylie grasped the situation in a flash. He turned reassuringly to the still panting Miss Counihan and said :

" Do not be alarmed, my dear. This is Cooper, Neary's man. He never knocks, nor sits, nor takes his hat off. No doubt he has news of Murphy."

" Oh, if you have," cried Miss Counihan, " if you have news of my love, speak, speak I adjure you." She was an omnivorous reader.

It was true that Cooper never sat, his acathisia was deep-seated and of long standing. It was indifferent to him whether he stood or lay, but sit he could not. From Euston to Holyhead he had stood, from Holyhead to Dun Laoghaire, lain. Now he stood again, bolt upright in the centre of the room, his bowler hat on his head, his scarlet choker tightly knotted, his glass eye bloodshot, sliding his middle fingers up and down the seams of his baggy moleskins just above the knee, saying, " I do be turned off, I do be turned off," over and over again.

" Rather say," said Wylie, who unlike Murphy preferred the poorest joke to none, provided it was he who made it, " you do be turned on."

He poured out a large whiskey and handed it to him, saying :

" This will help the needle off the crack."

The large whiskey was the merest smell of a cork to Cooper, who did not however turn up his nose at it on that account. Most of the corks he was offered were odourless.

Cooper's account, expurgated, accelerated, improved and reduced, of how he came to be turned off, gives the following.

After many days he picked up Murphy in the Cockpit late one afternoon and tracked him to the mew in West Brompton. At the corner of the mew a glorious gin-palace stood foursquare, a pub that had no need of the sun, neither of the moon, to shine upon it. As Cooper passed, hard on Murphy's heels, the grille parted, the shutters rolled up, the doors swung open. Cooper kept on his way, Murphy's way, until that ended in the house that Murphy entered. He let himself in, therefore he lived there. Cooper made a mental note of the number and hastened back the way he had come, devising as he went the wire to Neary.

At the corner he paused to admire the pub, superior to any he had ever seen. Suddenly a man was standing in the porch, radiant in his shirt-sleeves and an apron of fine baize, holding fast a bottle of whiskey. His face was as the face of an angel, he stretched out his hand upon Cooper.

When he came out five hours later his thirst was firmly established. The doors closed, the shutters rattled down, the wings of the grille came together. The defence of West Brompton, by West Brompton, against West Brompton, was taking no chances.

He raged, Pantagruel had him by the throat.

The moon, by a striking coincidence full and at perigee, bathed the palatial tantalus in an ironical radiance. He ground his jaws, he clenched fiercely the slack of his trouser knees, he was ripe for mischief. He thought of Murphy, his quarry, therefore his enemy. The door of the house was ajar, ne closed it behind him and stood in the dark hall. He struck a fusee. The one room opening off the hall was doorless, no sound nor light came from the basement. He climbed the stairs. He opened a door on the mezzanine, only to behold, in the eerie flicker of the fusee, an earth closet. Two rooms opened off the first-floor landing, one was doorless, a long gasp of despair issued from the other. Cooper entered, found Murphy in the appalling position described in section three, assumed that a murder had been bungled and retreated headlong. As he burst out of the door the most beautiful young woman he had ever seen slipped in.

" Alas ! " cried Miss Counihan. " False and cruel ! "

He took tube to Wapping, whose defence of itself, by itself, against itself, was less implacable than West Brompton's, and there drank for a week. His thirst and money ended together, a merciful coincidence. He rifled poor-box after poor-box until he had scraped together a few shillings. He hurried back to West Brompton, only pausing on the way to wire the good news to Neary, that Murphy was found. The ruins of the mew were being carted away, to make room for an architecture more in keeping with the palace on the corner. He hurried back to his stew, only pausing on the way to wire the bad news to Neary, that Murphy was lost.

Neary arrived the following morning. Cooper threw himself on his mercy, abated not one tittle of the truth and was turned off with contumely.

Some days later he was taken up for begging without singing and given ten days. The leisure hours of his confinement, which would otherwise have hung most heavy on his hands, he devoted to bringing up to date the return half of his monthly ticket, so that he might lose no time, the moment he was free, in returning to the dear land of his birth. He had been some days in Dublin, looking for Miss Counihan, who had not left an address at Wynn's Hotel. Now at last he found her, with pleased surprise in the arms of Mr. Wylie, whom of course he remembered from the G.P. days, those happy days now gone for ever. He wiped away a tear.

All the puppets in this book whinge sooner or later, except Murphy, who is not a puppet.

Wylie browbeat :

" Could you find Murphy again ? "

" Maybe," said Cooper.

" Could you find Neary ? "

" Handy," said Cooper.

" Did you know that Neary had deserted his wife ? "

" I did," said Cooper.

" Did you know she was in London ? "

" I did," said Cooper.

" Why didn't you go to her when Neary turned you off ? "

Cooper did not like this question at all. He presented his profiles, between which there was little resemblance, many times in rapid succession to his tormentor.

" Why not ? " said Wylie.

" I do be too fond of Mr. Neary," said Cooper.

" Liar," said Wylie.

This was not a question. Cooper waited for the next question.

" Neary knows too much," said Wylie.

Cooper waited.

" You split on him," said Wylie, " he splits on you. Isn't that it ? "

Cooper admitted nothing.

" All you need," said Wylie, " is a little kindness, and in a short time you will be sitting down and taking off your hat and doing all the things that are impossible at present. Miss Counihan and I are your friends."

Cooper could not have looked more gratified if he had been Frankenstein's dæmon and Wylie De Lacey.

" Now, Cooper," said Wylie, " will you be so kind as to leave the room and wait outside till I am so courteous as to call you ? "

Wylie's first care, when Cooper had left the room, was to kiss Miss Counihan's tears away. He had a special kiss for this purpose, an astringent kiss, with a movement like a barber's clippers. Not the thought of Murphy upside down and bleeding, but that of the beautiful female visitor, had upset Miss Counihan. Mindful of Neary's blunder by the grave of Father Prout (F. S. Mahony), Wylie pointed out that there was nothing whatever to connect Murphy with the young woman seen by Cooper on his way out. But Miss Counihan was offended, not mollified, by this suggestion, which seemed to her a disparagement of Murphy. For what could beauty's business be in Murphy's vicinity, if not with Murphy ? She increased the flow of tears, partly to show how offended she was, partly because the kisses she was now getting were quite a new experience.

When the effort of shedding tears finally became greater than the pleasure of having them kissed away, Miss Counihan discontinued it. Wylie restored himself with a little whiskey and gave out the following as his considered opinion, which indeed it was.

The time had come to remove, one way or another, once and for all, Miss Counihan's uncertainty, which was also that of her well-wishers, meaning himself. Neary without Cooper would never find Murphy. But even supposing he did, would Miss Counihan be in any way relieved? On the contrary. For if Murphy had not already of his own free imbecility turned down Miss Counihan in his mind, Neary would bully or bribe him into doing so in black and white, or, failing that, have him removed. A man capable of bigamous designs on Miss Counihan was capable of anything.

Even Wylie did not know of the first Mrs. Neary, alive and well, though officially languishing, in Calcutta.

"Though I hold no brief for Mr. Neary," said Miss Counihan, "yet I am loath to think he is the dastard you describe. If, as you say, on what grounds I do not inquire, he has deserted his wife, no doubt he had excellent reasons for doing so."

Miss Counihan could not think too harshly

of a man whom her charms had brought to the brink of bigamy, if indeed they had. Nor was any good purpose to be served by her concurring in Wylie's denigrations of a suitor more solvent, if—er—personally less interesting than himself. She would not identify herself more closely with Wylie than was convenient to her purpose (Murphy) or agreeable to her appetite. If she treated him with less rigour than she had Neary, it was simply because the latter took away her appetite. But she had made it as clear to the one as she had to the other, that so long as any hope of Murphy remained her affections were to be regarded as in a state of suspension. Wylie accepted this with a very good grace. He found her suspended affections so cordial that he did not greatly care if they were never released.

Wylie, intelligent enough to thank his stars he was not more so, saw his mistake in defending Murphy and attacking Neary. A man could no more work a woman out of position on her own ground of sentimental lech than he could outsmell a dog. Her instinct was a menstruum, resolving every move he made, immediately and without effort, into its final implications for her vanity and interest. The only points at which Miss Counihan was vulnerable were her erogenous

zones and her need for Murphy. He engaged
a rapid skirmish with the former and said :

" I may be quite wrong about Neary. I
trust I am. He may be the most dependable
person in the world. But without Cooper he
will never find Murphy. His talents are not
that kind. And till Murphy is found there is
nothing to be done."

Miss Counihan had a sad feeling that after
Murphy was found there might be still less to
be done. She said :

" What do you propose ? "

Before Wylie proposed anything he would
like to say that Murphy's need for Miss Counihan
was certainly greater than hers for him. She
could judge of his distress from Cooper's description of how he had found him, the victim
apparently of some brutal attack, at the hands
of a business rival in all probability, in a dwelling
not only unfit for human habitation but condemned by the central authority. Now he was
probably sleeping on the Embankment, or being
moved all night long round and round St.
James's Park, or suffering the agonies of the
damned in the crypt of St. Martin's in the
Fields. It was essential to find him without
delay, not merely in order to have him satisfy
Miss Counihan that his attitude towards her

was as positive as it had ever been, though that of course remained the paramount consideration, but also so that he might be saved from his foolish Irish pride. So long as he was allowed to deprive himself of Miss Counihan's society, through some mistaken idea of chivalry, his every effort was being crippled. But with Miss Counihan at his side, to stimulate, encourage, console and reward him, there was no eminence to which he might not attain.

"I asked what you proposed," said Miss Counihan.

Wylie proposed that they should all go to London, she, he and Cooper. She would be the heart and soul, he the brains, Cooper the claws, of the expedition. This would enable her to let loose on Murphy, the moment he was found, her pent-up affections, which he, Wylie, in the meantime, would be happy and flattered to exercise daily, in addition to his lesser functions of dealing with Neary and keeping Cooper off the bottle. And bringing hope into the life of Ariadne née Cox, he might have added, but did not.

"And who pays," said Miss Counihan, "for this big push?"

"Ultimately Neary," said Wylie.

He adduced the letter, in which Neary be-

moaned his hastiness with Cooper, implored
Wylie to enter his service, and panted after
the hem of Miss Counihan's fur coat, as one
of credit through and through. It might be
necessary to call on Miss Counihan for some
of the more immediate outgoings, which she
must regard not as a mere advance, but as an
investment, with Murphy among the dividends.

" I could not leave before Saturday," said
Miss Counihan. She was in the middle of a
fitting.

" Well," said Wylie, " the better the day . . .
It is always pleasant to leave this country, but
never more so than by the Saturday B. and I.,
with the ladies and gentlemen of the theatre
enjoying the high-seas licence and a full night
on the water."

" I mean there would be time," said Miss
Counihan, " to advise Mr. Neary and have
the whole arrangement placed on a less—er—
speculative footing."

" I am against any liaison with Neary," said
Wylie, " until Murphy is found. Applied to
now, with everything still so very much up in
the air, he might be foolish enough to put
obstacles in the way of his own advancement.
But confront him with his friend and beloved,
at a moment when his spirits are low, with

Murphy in the background an accomplished fact, and a shower of benefits is I think certain."

If the worst comes to the worst, thought Wylie, if Murphy cannot be found, if Neary turns nasty, there is always the Cox.

If the worst comes to the worst, thought Miss Counihan, if my love cannot be found, if Wylie turns nasty, there is always Neary.

"Very well," she said.

Wylie assured her she would never regret it. None of them would ever regret it. It was the beginning of new life for them all, her, Murphy, Neary, his unworthy self. It was the end of darkness for all concerned. He moved towards the door.

"Regret or not," said Miss Counihan, "new life or not, I shall never forget your kindness."

He stood with his back to the door, one hand behind him holding the handle, the other describing the gesture that he always used when words were inadequate to conceal what he felt. Miss Counihan in turn compelled just so much understanding to sit for a moment on her face as it could readily retrieve. It was a risk she did not often care to take.

"It is you who are good," said Wylie, "not I."

Left alone, she stirred the fire in vain. The

turf was truly Irish in its eleutheromania, it would not burn behind bars. She turned off the light, opened the window and leaned out. Is it its back that the moon can never turn to the earth, or its face? Which was worse, never to serve him whom she loved or perpetually those, one after the other, whom she scarcely disliked. These were knotty points. Wylie and Cooper appeared on the pavement, two tiny heads in the pillories of their shoulders (Murphy's figure). Then Cooper was suddenly in motion, jerking along in his frustrated run, expanding into full length as he receded. She did not heed the click of the street door slammed, warning her to take up a position worthy of being surprised by Wylie, but craned still further out and down till not more than half her person, and that half clear of the floor, remained in the room. Bounding the grey pavement, stretching away on either hand beneath the grey spans of steps, the areas made a fosse of darkness. The spikes of the railings were a fine saw edge, spurting light. Miss Counihan closed her eyes, which was unwise, and seemed likely to leave the room altogether when Wylie's hands, making two skilful handfuls of her breasts, drew her back to a more social vertigo.

8

It must have been while the chandlers were mocking Murphy that the shocking thing happened.

That day, Friday, October the 11th, after many days, Miss Carridge found her bread, it came bobbing back to her in the form of free samples of various sorts, shaving soap, scent, toilet soap, foot salts, bath cubes, dentifrice, deodorants and even depilatories. It is so easy to lose personal freshness. Miss Carridge had one incalculable advantage over most of her kind—insmell into her infirmity. She would not stink without a struggle, provided the struggle were not too expensive.

Highly elated, thoroughly scoured and anointed in every nook and corner, rashly glowing with the sense of being what she called " pristine ", Miss Carridge appeared to Celia with the cup of tea. Celia was standing at the window, looking out, in an attitude quite foreign to her.

" Come in," said Celia.

" Drink it before it curdles," said Miss Carridge.
Celia whirled round, exclaiming :

" Oh, Miss Carridge, is that you, I am so
worried about the old boy, there has not been
a move or a stir out of him all day." Her
agitation carried her away, she came and took
Miss Carridge by the arm.

" What nonsense," said Miss Carridge, " he
took in his tray and put it out as usual."

" That was hours ago," said Celia. " There
hasn't been a stir out of him since."

" Pardon me," said Miss Carridge, " I heard
him moving about as usual quite distinctly."

" But how could you have and not me ? " said
Celia.

" For the excellent reason," said Miss Carridge, " that you are not I." She paused for
this striking nominative to be admired. " Have
you forgotten the day I had to draw your attention to the plaster he was stamping down on
your head ? "

" But now I have got to expect it," said Celia,
" and listen for it, and this is the first time I
haven't heard it."

" What nonsense," said Miss Carridge. " What
you want——"

" No, no," said Celia, " not till I know."

Miss Carridge shrugged without pity and

turned to go, Celia clung to her arm. Miss Carridge sweated blessings on the unguents that made such cordiality possible, beads of gratification burst out all over her. Truly it is a tragic quality, that which the Romans called *caper*, particularly when associated with insmell.

"My poor child," said the virgin Miss Carridge, "how can I set your mind at rest?"

"By going up and looking," said Celia.

"I have strict orders never to disturb him," said Miss Carridge, "but I cannot bear to see you in such a state."

Celia was in a state indeed, trembling and ashen. The footsteps overhead had become part and parcel of her afternoon, with the rocking-chair and the vermigrade wane of light. An Ægean nightfall suddenly in Brewery Road could not have upset her more than this failure of the steps.

She stood at the foot of the stairs while Miss Carridge climbed them softly, listened at the door, knocked, knocked louder, pounded, rattled the handle, opened with her duplicate key, took a few steps in the room, then stood still. The old boy lay curled up in meanders of blood on her expensive lino, a cut-throat razor clutched in his hand and his throat cut in effect. With a calm that surprised her Miss Carridge surveyed the scene. It was so exactly what she would have expected, and must therefore at some time or other have imagined, that she felt no shock, or very little. She heard Celia call " What ? " She said to herself, if I call a doctor I must pay his fee, but if I call the police . . . The razor was closed, a finger was almost severed, a sudden black flurry filled the mouth. These details, which she could never have imagined, caused her gorge to rise, these and others too painful to record. She came speeding down the stairs one step at a time, her feet going so fast that she seemed on little caterpillar wheels, her forefinger sawing horribly at her craw for Celia's benefit. She slithered to a stop on the steps of the house and screeched for the police. She capered about in the street like a consternated ostrich, with strangled distracted rushes towards the York and Caledonian Roads in turn, embarrassingly equi-distant from the tragedy, tossing up her arms, undoing the good work of the samples, screeching for police aid. Her mind was so collected that she saw clearly the impropriety of letting it appear so. When neighbours and passers-by had assembled in sufficient numbers, she scuttled back to hold her door against them.

The police arrived and sent for a doctor. The doctor arrived and sent for an ambulance. The

ambulance arrived and the old boy was carried
down the stairs, past Celia stuck on the landing,
and put into it. This proved that he still lived,
for it is a misdemeanour to put a corpse, no
matter how fresh, into an ambulance. But to
take one out contravenes no law, by-law, section
or sub-section, and it was perfectly in order for
the old boy to consummate, as he did, his felony
on the way to the hospital.

Miss Carridge was not a penny out of pocket,
not one penny. The police, not she, had called
the doctor, therefore his fee was on them. The
bloody dilapidation of her lovely lino was amply
covered by the month's advance rent paid by
the old boy the day before. She had carried
off the whole affair in splendid style.

Murphy spent most of that night and the next
day and the next night expounding by way of
comfort to Celia, on and off, angrily, the unutter-
able benefits that would accrue, were already
accruing, to the old boy from his demise. This
was quite beside the point, for Celia was mourn-
ing, like all honest survivors, quite frankly for
herself. Yet it was not until the small hours of
the Sunday morning that he realised the irrelev-
ance of what he was doing, and furthermore its
spuriousness. So far from being adapted to
Celia, it was not addressed to her.

It is hard to say why she was, and remained, so profoundly distressed. The damage done to her afternoons, which she had grown to treasure almost as much as Murphy his before she picked him up, seems inadequate to account for it. She kept on wanting but not daring to go up and look at the room where it happened. She would go as far as the foot of the stairs and then come back. Her whole behaviour annoyed Murphy, of whose presence she seemed conscious only in fits and starts, and then with a kind of impersonal rapture that he did not relish in the least.

Finally his intimation, proudly casual, that a job was his or as good as his at last, excited her to the extent of an " Oh ". Nothing more. Not even an " Oh indeed ". He took her angrily by the shoulders and forced her to look at him. The clear green of her eyes, rolling now and everted like an aborting goat's, was silted with yellow.

" Look at me," he said.

She looked through him. Or back off him.

" Ever since June," he said, " it has been job, job, job, nothing but job. Nothing happens in the world but is specially designed to exalt me into a job. I say a job is the end of us both, or at least of me. You say no, but the beginning. I am to be a new man, you are to be a new woman, the entire sublunary excrement will turn to civet, there will be more joy in heaven over Murphy finding a job than over the billions of leather-bums that never had anything else. I need you, you only want me, you have the whip, you win."

He stopped, left in the lurch by his emotion. The anger that gave him the energy to begin was gone before he had half ended. A few words used it up. So it had always been, not only with anger, not only with words.

Celia did not look a winner, sagging under his hands, breathing painfully through her mouth, her eyes soiled and wild.

" Avoid exhaustion," she murmured, in weary ellipsis of Suk.

" I drag round this warren," said Murphy, with the last dregs of resentment, " day after day, hail, rain, sleet, snow, sog, I mean fog, soot, and I suppose fine, my breeches falling off with a fourpenny vomitory, looking for *your* job. At last I find it, it finds me, I am half dead with abuse and exposure, I am in a marasmus, I do not delay a moment but come crawling back to receive your congratulations. You say ' Oh '. It is better than ' Yah '."

" You don't understand," said Celia, who was not trying to follow.

" No," said Murphy. " A decayed valet severs

the connexion and you set up a niobaloo as though he were your fourteen children. No. I am at a loss."

" Not valet," said Celia. " Butler. Ex-butler."

" XX butler," said Murphy. " Porter."

The little scene was over, if scene it could be called. There was a long silence, Celia forgiving Murphy for having spoken roughly to her, Miss Counihan, Wylie and Cooper breaking their fast on the Liverpool–London express. Murphy got up and began to dress with care.

" Why did the barmaid champagne ? " he said. " Do you give it up ? "

" Yes," said Celia.

" Because the stout porter bitter," said Murphy.

This was a joke that did not amuse Celia, at the best of times and places it could not have amused her. That did not matter. So far from being adapted to her, it was not addressed to her. It amused Murphy, that was all that mattered. He always found it most funny, more than most funny, clonic, it and one other concerning a bottle of stout and a card party. These were the Gilmigrim jokes, so called from the Lilliputian wine. He staggered about on the floor in his bare feet, one time amateur theological student's shirt, dicky and lemon bow, overcome by the

toxins of this simple little joke. He sank down
on the dream of Descartes linoleum, choking and
writhing like a chicken with the gapes, seeing
the scene. On the one hand the barmaid, fresh
from the country, a horse's head on a cow's
body, her crape bodice more a W than a V, her
legs more an X than an O, her eyes closed for
the sweet pain, leaning out through the hatch of
the bar parlour. On the other the stout porter,
mounting the footrail, his canines gleaming
behind a pad of frothy whisker. Then the nip,
and Tintoretto's *Origin of the Milky Way.*

The fit was so much more like one of epilepsy
than of laughter that Celia felt alarm. Watching
him roll on the floor in his only decent shirt and
dicky, she made the needful changes, recalled the
scene in the mew and went to his assistance, as
she had then. It was unnecessary, the fit was
over, gloom took its place, as after a heavy
night.

He suffered her to dress him. When she had
done he sat down in his chair and said :

" God knows now when I'll be back."

Immediately she wanted to know all about it.
It was in order to torment at his ease this tardy
concern that he had sat down. He still loved
her enough to enjoy cutting the tripes out of her
occasionally. When he felt appeased, as he soon

did, he stopped rocking, held up his hand and said :

"The job is your fault. If it doesn't come off I'll be back this evening. If it does come off I don't know when I'll be back. That was what I meant when I said God knew. If they let me start straight away so much the worse."

"They ? " said Celia. "Who ? Start what ? "

"You'll know this evening," said Murphy. "Or if not this evening, to-morrow evening. Or if not to-morrow evening, the day after to-morrow evening. And so on." He stood up. "Give the coat a bit of a dinge behind in the waist," he said. "The draught is terrible."

She made a long dent in the waist of the coat. In vain, it filled out again immediately, as a punctured ball will not retain an impression.

"It won't stay," she said.

Murphy sighed.

"It is the second childhood," he said. "Hard on the heels of the pantaloons."

He kissed her, in Lydian mode, and went to the door.

"I believe you're leaving me," said Celia.

"Perhaps for just a little while you compel me to," said Murphy.

"For good and all."

"Oh no," he said, "only for just a little while

at the maximum. If for good and all I would take the chair." He felt in his pocket to make sure he had Suk. He had. He went.

She was too undressed to see him off at the door, she had to be content with standing on a chair and putting her head out of the window. She was beginning to wonder why he did not appear when he came back into the room.

" Wasn't there to be an execution this morning ? " he said.

" Never on Sunday," said Celia.

He struck his head despairingly, shook it and went again. He knew perfectly well the day was Sunday, it was essential that it should be, and yet he kept on thinking it was Friday, day of execution, love and fast.

From the window she saw him stand irresolute at the gate, his head sunk in the pillory of his shoulders, holding the coat in against his waist before and behind, as though turned to stone in the middle of a hornpipe. After a time he moved off in the direction of York Road, but stopped after a few steps and stood against the railings, gripping the neck of a spike at his head, in the attitude of one leaning on a staff.

When all the other circumstances of this departure had become blunted in her mind she continued to see, at the most unexpected times,

whether she would or no, the hand clutching the
spike of railing, the fingers loosening and tighten-
ing, higher than the dark head.

He retraced his steps slowly, hissing. Celia
thought he was coming back for something he
had forgotten, but no. As he passed the door,
going towards Pentonville, she called down good-
bye. He did not hear her, he was hissing.

His figure so excited the derision of a group
of boys playing football in the road that they
stopped their game. She watched him multiplied
in their burlesque long after her own eyes could
see him no more.

He did not return that night, nor the next,
nor the next. On Monday Miss Carridge asked
where he was. " Away on business," said Celia.
On Tuesday Miss Carridge asked when she
expected him back. " From day to day," said
Celia. On Wednesday Miss Carridge received
a new lot of samples and brought up the tea.
" Will you sit down ? " said Celia. " Most
happy," said Miss Carridge. Well she might
be.

" Are you in trouble ? " said Miss Carridge,
whose charity stopped at nothing short of alms.
" Of course, you know your own business best,
but I hear you moving about in the afternoon

just like the old boy, God Almighty rest his immortal soul, before he was taken from us."

This striking use of the passive voice did not spring from any fatalistic notions in the mind of Miss Carridge, but from her conviction, which as the landlady she felt it her duty to hold and utter as often as possible, that the old boy had cut his throat by accident.

" Oh no," said Celia, " no special trouble."

" Ah well, we all have our troubles," said Miss Carridge, sighing, wishing her own were a little less penetrating.

" Tell me about the old boy," said Celia.

The story that Miss Carridge had to tell was very pathetic and tedious. It brightened up a little with her reconstruction of the death scene, cupidity lending wings to her imagination.

" He gets out his razor to shave, as he always did regular about noon." A lie. The old boy shaved once a week and then the last thing at night. " That I do know, because I found the brush on the dresser with a squeeze of paste on top." A lie. " He goes to put up the tube before he lathers, he walks across the room with the razor in his hand, screwing the cap on the tube. He drops the cap, he throws the tube on the bed and goes down on the floor. I found the tube on the bed and the cap under the bed."

Lies. " He goes crawling about the floor, with the razor open in his hand, when all of a sudden he has a seizure." Pronounced on the analogy of manure. " He told me when he first came he might have a seizure any minute, he had two this year already, one on Shrove Tuesday, the other on Derby Day. That I do know." All lies. " He falls on his face with the razor under him, zzzeeeppp ! " she reinforced the onomatopœia with dumb-show, " what more do you want ? "

It was not for this that Celia had put Miss Carridge on to the old boy. She looked pleasant and waited.

" What I say is this," said Miss Carridge, " and it's what I said to the c'roner. A man doesn't pay a month's advance rent one day and do away with himself the next. It isn't natural." She really convinced herself with this argument. " Now if he was in arrears I wouldn't be so sure."

Celia agreed that to owe Miss Carridge rent would be a dreadful situation.

" What did they say at the inquest ? " said Celia.

" *Felo-de-se*," said Miss Carridge, with scorn and anger, " and got the room a bad name all over Islington. God knows now when I'll get it off. *Felo-de-se* ! Felo-de my rump." Just like Mr. Kelly.

Here at last was the opening that Celia had been waiting for. The fact that Miss Carridge had made it, and not she, gave an almost charitable air to what she had to propose.

She and Murphy would go upstairs and leave their room, to which no sinister associations attached, free for letting.

" My dear child ! " ejaculated Miss Carridge, and waited for the catch.

They would be willing to pay for the room alone what the old boy had paid for the room and his keep, which worked out monthly at ten shillings less than what they paid at present, as Miss Carridge in a moment of gush had had the folly to reveal. The room was on the small side for two, but Mr. Murphy expected to be away more than formerly and they would be glad of the saving.

" Hah ! " said Miss Carridge. " Saving ? Then am I to take it you expect me to send the same bill to Mr. Quigley and hand you over the ten bob ? "

" Less the usual commission," said Celia.

" This is most insulting," said Miss Carridge, racking her brains for a means of making it less so.

" How ? " said Celia. " Mr. Quigley will be no worse off. You are the victim of circumstances. You must live. We oblige you, you oblige us."

Celia's professional powers of persuasion had been dulled by her association with Murphy. What revived them now was not any desire to succeed with Miss Carridge where he had failed, but an immense longing to get into the old boy's room.

"That may be," said Miss Carridge, "but it is the principle of the thing, the principle of the thing." Her face took on an expression of intense concentration, almost of anguish. To accommodate the principle of such a transaction to her sense of what was honourable would take a little time, a little prayer and possibly even meditation.

"I must go and ask for guidance," she said.

After a decent interval for a thorough self-scrutiny, during which Celia packed, Miss Carridge came back, her face serene. There remained just one small matter to regulate before the process of mutual assistance could begin, namely, the precise meaning of "usual commission".

"Ten per cent," said Celia.

"Twelve and a half," said Miss Carridge.

"Very well," said Celia. "I cannot haggle."

"Nor I," said Miss Carridge.

" If you can manage the two bags," said
Celia, " I can manage the chair."

" Is that all you've got ? " said Miss Carridge
contemptuously. She was annoyed at Celia's
having taken the divine indulgence for granted.

" All," said Celia.

The old boy's room was half as big as theirs,
half as high, twice as bright. The walls and
linoleum were the same. The bed was tiny.
Miss Carridge could not imagine how the two of
them were ever going to manage. When not
fired by cupidity, Miss Carridge's imagination
was of the feeblest.

" I know I shouldn't like to sleep two in it,"
she said.

Celia opened the window.

" I expect Mr. Murphy to be away a great
deal," she said.

" Ah well," said Miss Carridge, " we all have
our troubles."

Celia unpacked her bag, but not Murphy's.
It was late afternoon. She got out of her clothes
and into the rocking-chair. Now the silence
above was a different silence, no longer strangled.
The silence not of vacuum but of plenum, not
of breath taken but of quiet air. The sky. She
closed her eyes and was in her mind with Murphy,
Mr. Kelly, clients, her parents, others, herself a

girl, a child, an infant. In the cell of her mind, teasing the oakum of her history. Then it was finished, the days and places and things and people were untwisted and scattered, she was lying down, she had no history.

It was a most pleasant sensation. Murphy did not come back to curtail it.

Penelope's curriculum was reversed, the next day and the next it was all to do over again, the coils of her life to be hackled into tow all over again, before she could lie down in the paradisial innocence of days and places and things and people. Murphy did not come back to expel her.

The next day was Saturday (if our reckoning is correct) and Miss Carridge announced that the char was coming to do out the big room and might as well do out the old boy's room as well. They both continued to think and speak of the top room as the old boy's room. While the char was doing it out Celia could wait below in the big room. "Or downstairs with me if you prefer," said Miss Carridge, with pitiable diffidence.

"That is very good of you," said Celia.

"Most happy," said Miss Carridge.

"But I think I ought to get out," said Celia. She had not been outside the door for more than a fortnight.

" Please yourself," said Miss Carridge.

On the steps of the house Celia departing met
the char arriving. Celia set off towards Pentonville, with the swagger that could not be disguised.
The char stared after her at length, gave her nose
a long wipe and through it said, though there
was none to hear :

" Lovely work, if you can get it."

Her course was clear : the Round Pond. The
temptation to revisit West Brompton was strong,
to tread her old beat in the daylight, to stand
again at the junction of Cremorne Road and
Stadium Street, to see the barges of waste paper
on the river and the funnels vailing to the bridges,
but she set it aside. There would be time for
that. There was a good breeze from the west,
she would go and watch Mr. Kelly sailing his
kite.

She took the Piccadilly tube from Caledonian
Road to Hyde Park Corner and walked along
the grass north of the Serpentine. Each leaf as
it fell had an access of new life, a sudden frenzy
of freedom at contact with the earth, before it
lay down with the others. She had meant to
cross the water by Rennie's Bridge and enter
Kensington Gardens by one of the wickets in the
eastern boundary, but remembering the dahlias
at Victoria Gate she changed her mind and bore

off to the right into the north, round the accident
house of the Royal Humane Society.

Cooper was standing under a tree in the Cockpit, as he had done, with spells of lying, all day
and every day since his return to London with
Wylie and Miss Counihan. He recognised Celia
as she swaggered past. He let her get well ahead
and then started after her, his gait more frustrated
than ever as he forced himself to keep his distance.
He could not help gaining on her, he had to
stop every now and then to let her get on. She
stood a long time before the dahlias, then entered
the gardens by the fountains. She took the path
straight across to the Round Pond, walked round
it clockwise and sat down on a bench on the west
side with her back to the palace and the wind,
close to the flyers, but not too close. She wanted
to see Mr. Kelly, but not to be seen by him.
Not yet.

The flyers were some old men, most of whom
she recognised from the days when she had come
regularly with Mr. Kelly every Saturday afternoon, and one child. Mr. Kelly was late.

It began to rain, she moved into the shelter.
A young man followed her, pleasantly spoken,
amorously disposed. She could not blame him,
it was a natural mistake, she felt sorry for him,
she disabused him gently.

The water splashed over the margin of the pond, the nearer kites were writhing and plunging. The nearer they were, the more contorted and wild. One came down in the pond. Another, after prolonged paroxysms, behind the cast of the Physical Energy of G. F. Watts, O.M., R.A. Only two rode steadily, a tandem, coupled abreast like the happy tug and barge, flown by the child from a double winch. She could just discern them, side by side high above the trees, specks against the east darkening already. The wrack broke behind them as she watched, for a moment they stood out motionless and black, in a glade of limpid viridescent sky.

She grew more and more impatient for Mr. Kelly to come and show his skill as the chances of his doing so diminished. She sat on till it was nearly dark and all the flyers, except the child, had gone. At last he also began to wind in and Celia watched for the kites to appear. When they did their contortions surprised her, she could hardly believe it was the same pair that had ridden so serenely on a full line. The child was expert, he played them with a finesse worthy of Mr. Kelly himself. In the end they came quietly, hung low in the murk almost directly overhead, then settled gently. The child knelt down in the rain, dismantled them, wrapped the tails and sticks in the sails and went away, singing. As he passed the shelter Celia called good night. He did not hear her, he was singing.

Soon the gates would close, all over the gardens the rangers were crying their cry : *All out.* Celia started slowly up the Broad Walk, wondering what could have happened to Mr. Kelly, impervious in the ordinary way to every form of weather except the dead calm. It was not as though he depended on her to wheel him, he always insisted on propelling the chair himself. He enjoyed the sensation of plying the levers, he said it was like working the pulls of a beer-engine. It looked as though something were amiss with Mr. Kelly.

She took the District Railway from Notting Hill Gate to King's Cross. So did Cooper. She toiled up Caledonian Road, feeling the worse for her outing. She was tired and wet, Mr. Kelly had failed, the child had ignored her good night. There was nothing to go back to, yet she was glad when she arrived. So was Cooper. She let herself in, therefore she lived there. This time he did not exceed his instructions, but hastened away as soon as he had made a mental note of the number. Cooper's mental notes were few, but ineffaceable. Celia had begun to climb the stairs in the dark when Miss Carridge came

out of her room and switched on the light.
Celia stopped, her feet on different steps, her
hand on the banister, her face in profile.

" Mr. Murphy came while you were out," said
Miss Carridge. " You can't have been gone five
minutes."

For a full second Celia mistook this to mean
that Murphy had come back.

" He took his bag and the chair," said Miss
Carridge, " but couldn't wait."

There was the usual silence, Miss Carridge
missing nothing of Celia's expression, Celia
appearing to scrutinise her hand on the banister.

" Any message," said Celia, at last.

" I can't hear you," said Miss Carridge.

" Did Mr. Murphy leave any message ? " said
Celia, turning away and taking another step
upward.

" Wait now till I see," said Miss Carridge.
Celia waited.

" Yes," said Miss Carridge, " now that you
ask me, he did say to tell you he was all right
and would be writing." A lie. Miss Carridge's
pity knew no bounds but alms.

When it was quite clear that this was the whole
extent of the message Celia went on slowly up
the stairs. Miss Carridge stood with a finger on
the switch, watching. The turn of the stair took

the body out of sight, but Miss Carridge could still see the hand on the banister, gripping, then sliding a little, gripping again, then sliding a little more. When the hand also disappeared Miss Carridge switched off the light and stood in the dark that was so much less extravagant, not to mention richer in acoustic properties, listening.

She heard with surprise the door of the big room opened and closed again immediately. After a pause the steps resumed their climb, no more slowly than before, but perhaps a little less surely. She waited till she heard the old boy's door close, neither loudly nor softly, and then went back to her book : *The Candle of Vision*, by George Russell (A.E.).

9

Il est difficile à celui qui vit hors du monde de ne pas rechercher les siens. (MALRAUX)

THE Magdalen Mental Mercyseat lay a little way out of town, ideally situated in its own grounds on the boundary of two counties. In order to die in the one sheriffalty rather than in the other some patients had merely to move up, or be moved up, a little in the bed. This sometimes proved a great convenience.

The head male nurse, Mr. Thomas ("Bim") Clinch, a huge red, bald, whiskered man of overweening ability and authority in his own department, had a fancy for Ticklepenny not far short of love. It was largely thanks to this that Ticklepenny had been taken on in the first place. It was largely thanks to it now that Murphy was taken on in Ticklepenny's stead. For Ticklepenny had vowed to Bim that if Murphy were not taken on in his stead, to release him from the torments of the wards, he would go, pay or no pay. But if Murphy were taken on he would stay, he would return to the bottles and the slops and so remain available for Bim's fancy, which was not far short of love.

After a sharp struggle between man and head male nurse Bim neatly reconciled his pleasure and his duty. He would take Murphy on a month's probation and release Ticklepenny from his contract. When Murphy had completed his month, and not before, Ticklepenny would be paid for the ten days he had served. Thus Ticklepenny was made security for Murphy and the fancy given a full month in which to cloy.

Ticklepenny proposed that he should be paid his ten days as soon as Murphy had completed, not his own month, but as much of Ticklepenny's as had still to run.

" Darling," said Bim, " you will get your one-six-eight as soon as your Murphy has given a month's satisfaction and no sooner."

" Then make it one-ten," said Ticklepenny. " Have a heart."

" That is entirely up to you," said Bim.

Thus Murphy's appointment, as though to a position of the highest trust, was a foregone conclusion. His own merits were so recondite, in spite of the magical eye, that he obviously could not be appointed on them, but only on the demerits, or by-merits, of Ticklepenny. So it was that a few minutes after his arrival he found himself being signed on and admonished by Bim, who did not like the look of him in the least.

He would be expected to make beds, carry trays, clean up regular messes, clean up casual messes, read thermometers, write charts, wash the bedridden, give medicine, hound down its effects, warm bedpans, cool fevers, boil gags, sterilize when in doubt, honour and obey the male sister, wait hand, foot and mouth on the doctor when he came, look pleasant.

He would never lose sight of the fact that he was dealing with patients not responsible for what they did or said.

He would never on any account allow himself to be affected by the abuse, no matter how foul and unmerited, that would be poured out upon him. The patients seeing so much of the nurses and so little of the doctor, it was natural that they should regard the former as their persecutors and the latter as their saviour.

He would never on any account be rough with a patient. Restraint and coercion were sometimes unavoidable, but must always be exerted with the utmost tenderness. After all it was a mercyseat. If singlehanded he could

not handle a patient without hurting him, let
him call the other nurses to his assistance.

He would never lose sight of the fact that he
was a creature without initiative. He had no
competence to register facts on his own account.
There were no facts in the M.M.M. except those
sanctioned by the doctor. Thus, to take a simple
example, when a patient died suddenly and
flagrantly, as was sometimes bound to happen
even in the M.M.M., let him assume nothing of
the kind when sending for the doctor. No
patient was dead till the doctor had seen him.

He would never on any account neglect to
keep his mouth shut. The mercies of the Mercyseat were private and confidential.

These were the main points to be kept constantly in mind. Other routine details would be
explained to him as he went along.

He was assigned to Skinner's House, male side,
first floor. His hours would be 8 to 12 and 2 to 8.
He would start the following morning. He
would be on day duty the first week, on night
duty the second week. The peculiar features of
night duty would be explained to him when the
time came.

A less remarkable outfit would be issued to him.

Had he any questions before he was passed on
to Ticklepenny?

There was a silence, Bim liking the look of Murphy less and less, Murphy racking his brains for a plausible curiosity.

" In that case——" said Bim.

" Are they all certified ? " said Murphy.

" That is not your business," said Bim. " You are not paid to take an interest in the patients, but to fetch for them, carry for them and clean up after them. All you know about them is the work they give you to do. Make no mistake about it."

Murphy learned later that about 15 per cent of the patients were certified, a little band select only in name, treated with exactly the same sanguine punctilio as the 85 per cent that were not certified. For the M.M.M. was a sanatorium, not a madhouse nor a home for defectives, and as such admitted only those cases whose prognoses were not hopeless. If the effect of treatment was to render the prognosis hopeless, as was sometimes bound to happen even in the M.M.M., then out went the patient, except in very special extenuating circumstances. Thus if the chronic (the soft impairment having been admitted) was a really charming chap, quiet, clean, biddable and solvent, he might be allowed to settle down in the M.M.M. for the rest of his natural. There were a few such fortunate cases, certified and uncertified, enjoying all the amenities of a mental hospital, from peraldehyde to slosh, without any of its therapeutic vexations.

Cringing with relief, Ticklepenny took Murphy first to his sleeping quarters, then to Skinner House.

Two large buildings, one for males, the other for females, remote from the main block and still more so from each other, housed the nursing staff and other menials. Married nurses, both male and female, lived out. No female nurse had taken a male nurse to husband within living memory, though one had once been almost obliged to.

Murphy had the choice of sharing a room with Ticklepenny or having a garret to himself. They climbed the ladder to the latter and Murphy chose it with such decision that even Ticklepenny felt a little slighted. It was not usual for Ticklepenny to feel slighted at all, it was unprecedented for him to do so without cause, as was the present case. For had he been Cleopatra herself, in the last years of her father's reign, Murphy would have made the same choice.

The reason for this eccentricity does not seem a very good one. Fewer years ago than he cared to remember, while still in the first cyanosis of youth, Murphy had occupied a garret in Hanover, not for long, but for long enough to experience all its advantages. Since then he had sought high and low for another, even half as good. In vain. What passed for a garret in Great Britain and Ireland was really nothing more than an attic. An attic! How was it possible for such a confusion to arise? A basement was better than an attic. An attic!

But the garret that he now saw was not an attic, nor yet a mansarde, but a genuine garret, not half, but twice as good as the one in Hanover, because half as large. The ceiling and the outer wall were one, a superb surge of white, pitched at the perfect angle of furthest trajectory, pierced by a small frosted skylight, ideal for closing against the sun by day and opening by night to the stars. The bed, so low and gone in the springs that even unfreighted the middle grazed the ground, was wedged lengthways into the cleft of floor and ceiling, so that Murphy was saved the trouble of moving it into that position. The garret contained, in addition to the bed, one chair and one chest, not of drawers. An immense candle, stuck to the floor by its own tallow, pointed its snuff to heaven at the head of the bed. This, the only means of light, was more than enough for Murphy, a strict non-reader. But he objected very strongly to there being no means of heat.

"I must have fire," he said to Ticklepenny, "I cannot live without fire."

Ticklepenny was sorry, he thought it most unlikely that Murphy would be granted a fire in the garret. There were no tubes or wires to that remote aery. A brazier seemed the only chance, but Bim would hardly allow a brazier. Murphy would find that a fire was really unnecessary in so confined a space. The flame within would work up a fine fug in no time.

"I come here to oblige you," said Murphy, "and I am still prepared to do so, but not without fire."

He went on to speak of tubes and wires. Was it not just the beauty of tubes and wires, that they could be extended? Was it not their chief characteristic, the ease with which they could be extended? What was the point of going in for tubes and wires at all, if you did not extend them without compunction whenever necessary? Did they not cry out for extension? Ticklepenny thought he would never stop, saying feverishly the same thing in slightly different ways.

"You should see my fire," said Ticklepenny.

This infuriated Murphy. Was he to find a garret after all these years, just as all hope seemed dead, a garret that was actually not an attic, nor a mansarde, only to lose it again at once for want of a few yards of tube or wire? He broke into sweat, lost all his yellow, his heart pounded, the garret spun round, he could not speak. When he could he said, in a voice new to Ticklepenny :

" Have fire in this garret before night or——"

He stopped because he could not go on. It was an aposiopesis of the purest kind. Ticklepenny supplied the missing consequences in various versions, each one more painful than any that Murphy could have specified, terrifying taken all together. Suk's indication of silence as one of Murphy's highest attributes could not have been more strikingly justified.

It seems strange that neither of them thought of an oil-stove, say a small Valor Perfection. Bim could hardly have objected and all the trouble with tubes and wires would have been avoided. The fact remains that the idea of an oil-stove did not occur to either of them at the time, though it did long afterwards to Ticklepenny.

" Now for the wards," said Ticklepenny.

" Did you catch what I said," said Murphy, " by any chance? "

" I'll do what I can," said Ticklepenny.

" It makes no difference to me," said Murphy,
" whether I go or stay."

He was mistaken.

On the way to Skinner's House they passed a
bijou edifice of mellow brick with a forecourt of
lawn and flowers, its facade a profusion of
traveller's joy and self-clinging ampelopsis, set
in a bay of clipped yews.

" Is that the nursery ? " said Murphy.

" No," said Ticklepenny, " the mortuary."

Skinner's was a long, grey, two-storied building, dilated at both ends like a double obelisk.
The females were thrown all together to the west,
the males to the east, and on the strength of this
it was called a mixed house, as distinct from the
two convalescent houses, which very properly
were not mixed. Similarly, some public baths
are called mixed where the bathing is not.

Skinner's was the cockpit of the M.M.M. and
here the battle raged most fiercely, whenever it
could be engaged, between the psychotic and
psychiatric points of view. Patients left Skinner's
better, dead or chronic, for a convalescent house,
the mortuary or the exit, as the case might be.

They mounted directly to the first floor and
Murphy was submitted to the male sister, Mr.
Timothy (" Bom ") Clinch, younger twin and
dead spit of Bim. Bom, primed by Bim,

expected nothing from Murphy, and Murphy, *ex hypothesi*, nothing from Bom, with the result that neither was disappointed.

Bim Clinch had no fewer than seven male relations, linear and collateral, serving under him, of whom the greatest was Bom and perhaps the least an aged uncle (" Bum ") in the bandage-winding department, as well as an elder sister, two nieces and a by-blow on the female side. There was nothing old-fashioned or half-hearted about the nepotism of Bim Clinch, there was no more resolute and successful pope to his family in the south of England, and even in the south of Ireland there were still some who might have studied his methods with profit.

" This way," said Bom.

The wards consisted of two long corridors, intersecting to form a T, or more correctly a decapitated potence, the three extremities developed into spacious crutch-heads, which were the reading-, writing- and recreation-rooms or " wrecks ", known to the wittier ministers of mercy as the sublimatoria. Here the patients were encouraged to play billiards, darts, ping-pong, the piano and other less strenuous games, or simply to hang about doing nothing. The great majority preferred simply to hang about doing nothing.

To adopt for a moment as a purely descriptive

convenience the terms and orientation of church architecture, the layout of the wards was that of nave and transepts, with nothing east of the crossing. There were no open wards in the ordinary sense, but single rooms, or as some would say, cells, or as Boswell said, mansions, opening south off the nave and east and west off the transepts. North of the nave were the kitchens, patients' refectory, nurses' refectory, drug arsenal, patients' lavatory, nurses' lavatory, visitors' lavatory, etc. The bedridden and more refractory cases were kept together as far as possible in the south transept, off which opened the padded cells, known to the wittier as the " quiet rooms ", " rubber rooms " or, in a notable clip, " pads ". The whole place was overheated and stank of peraldehyde and truant sphincters.

There were not many patients about as Murphy followed Bom through the wards. Some were at matins, some in the gardens, some could not get up, some would not, some simply had not. But those that he did see were not at all the terrifying monsters that might have been imagined from Ticklepenny's account. Melancholics, motionless and brooding, holding their heads or bellies according to type. Paranoids, feverishly covering sheets of paper with complaints against their treatment or verbatim reports of their inner voices. A hebephrenic playing the piano intently. A hypomanic teaching slosh to a Korsakow's syndrome. An emaciated schizoid, petrified in a toppling attitude as though condemned to an eternal *tableau vivant*, his left hand rhetorically extended holding a cigarette half smoked and out, his right, quivering and rigid, pointing upward.

They caused Murphy no horror. The most easily identifiable of his immediate feelings were respect and unworthiness. Except for the manic, who was like an epitome of all the self-made plutolaters who ever triumphed over empty pockets and clean hands, the impression he received was of that self-immersed indifference to the contingencies of the contingent world which he had chosen for himself as the only felicity and achieved so seldom.

The tour being over and all Bim's precepts exemplified, Bom led the way back to the crossing and said :

" That is all now. Report in the morning at eight."

He waited to be thanked before he opened the door. Ticklepenny nudged Murphy.

" A million thanks," said Murphy.

" Don't thank me," said Bom. " Any questions ? "

Murphy knew better, but made a show of consulting with himself.

" He would like to start in straight away," said Ticklepenny.

" That is a matter for Mr. Tom," said Mr. Tim.

" Oh, it's all O.K. with Mr. Tom," said Ticklepenny.

" My instructions are he doesn't come on till the morning," said Bom.

Ticklepenny nudged Murphy, this time unnecessarily. For Murphy was only too anxious to test his striking impression that here was the race of people he had long since despaired of finding. Also he wanted Ticklepenny to be free to rig up his fire. He would have played up unprompted.

" Of course I know my month only counts from to-morrow," he said, " but Mr. Clinch very kindly had no objection to my starting in straight away if I wanted to."

" And do you ? " said Bom, very incredulous, having seen the nudge (the second nudge).

" What he wants——" said Ticklepenny.

" You," said Bom with a sudden ferocity that put Murphy's heart across him, " you shut your bloody choke, we all know what you want." He mentioned one or two of the things that Ticklepenny most wanted. Ticklepenny wiped his face. Two sorts of reprimand were familiar to Ticklepenny, those that left him in the necessity of wiping his face and those that did not. He used no other principle of differentiation.

" Yes," said Murphy, " I should like very much to start in at once, if I might."

Bom gave up. When the fool supports the knave the good man may fold his hands. The fool in league with the knave against himself is a combination that none may withstand. Oh, monster of humanity and enlightenment, despairing of a world in which the only natural allies are the fools and knaves, a mankind sterile with self-complicity, admire Bom feeling dimly for once what you feel acutely so often, Pilate's hands rustling in his mind.

Thus Bom released Ticklepenny and delivered Murphy to his folly.

Feeling just the same old Wood's halfpenny in the regulation shirt and suit, perhaps because he refused to leave off the lemon bow, Murphy reported to Bom at two o'clock and entered upon that experience from which already he hoped for better things, without exactly knowing why or what things or in what way better.

He was sorry when eight o'clock came and he was sent off duty, having been loudly abused by

Bom for his clumsiness in handling things (trays, beds, thermometers, syringes, pans, jacks, spatulas, screws, etc.) and silently commended for his skill in handling the patients themselves, whose names and more flagrant peculiarities he had fully co-ordinated by the end of the six hours, what he might expect from them and what never hope.

Ticklepenny was lying all over the garret floor, struggling with a tiny old-fashioned gas radiator, firing a spark-pistol with a kind of despair, in the light of the candle. He related how the crazy installation had developed, step by step, typically, from the furthest-fetched of visions to a reality that would not function.

It had taken him an hour to perfect the vision. It had taken him another hour to unearth the radiator, the key-piece of the whole contraption, with spark-pistol ironically attached.

" I should have thought," said Murphy, " that the radiator was secondary to the gas."

He had brought the radiator to the garret, set it down on the floor and stood back to imagine it lit. Rusty, dusty, derelict, the coils of asbestos falling to pieces, it seemed to defy ignition. He went dismally away to look for gas.

It had taken him another hour to find what might be made to serve, a disused jet in the w.c., now lit by electricity, on the floor below.

The extremes having thus been established, nothing remained but to make them meet. This was a difficulty whose fascinations were familiar to him from the days when as a pot poet he had laboured so long and so lovingly to join the ends of his pentameters. He solved it in less than two hours by means of a series of discarded feed tubes eked out with cæsuræ of glass, thanks to which gas was now being poured into the radiator. Yet the asbestos would not kindle, pepper it with sparks as he might.

"You speak of gas," said Murphy, "but I smell no gas."

This was where he was at a disadvantage, for Ticklepenny did smell gas, faintly but distinctly. He described how he had turned it on in the w.c. and raced it back to the garret. He explained how the flow could only be regulated from the w.c., as there was no tap and no provision for a tap at the radiator's seat of entry. That was perhaps the chief inconvenience of his machine. A more dignified way for Murphy to light his fire, in default of an assistant to turn on the gas below while he waited above ready with the spark-pistol, would be to fix an asbestos nozzle on his end of the connexion, descend with this to the source of supply, light up in the w.c. and carry the fire back to the radiator at

his leisure. Or if he preferred he could bring
the whole radiator down to the w.c. and to hell
with a special nozzle. But those were minor
points. The main point was that he, Ticklepenny, had turned on the gas more than ten
minutes before and been firing sparks into the
radiator ever since, without result. This was
true.

" Either the gas is not on," said Murphy, " or
the connexion is broken."

" Amn't I after trying? " said Ticklepenny.
A lie. Ticklepenny was worn out.

" Try again," said Murphy. " Show me the
sparks."

Ticklepenny crawled down the ladder.
Murphy crouched before the radiator. In a
moment came a faint hiss, then a faint smell.
Murphy averted his head and pulled the trigger.
The radiator lit with a sigh and blushed, with
as much of its asbestos as had not perished.

" How's that? " called Ticklepenny from the
foot of the ladder.

Murphy went down, to prevent Ticklepenny,
whose immediate usefulness seemed over, from
coming up and to be shown the tap.

" Is she going? " said Ticklepenny.

" Yes," said Murphy. " Where's the tap? "

" Well, that beats all," said Ticklepenny.

What beat all was how the tap, which he really had turned on, came to be turned off.

The dismantled jet projected high up in the wall of the w.c. and what Ticklepenny called the tap was one of those double chain and ring arrangements designed for the convenience of dwarfs.

" As I hope to be saved," said Ticklepenny, " I swear I turned the little b—— on."

" Perhaps a little bird flew in," said Murphy, " and lit on it."

" How could he with the window shut ? " said Ticklepenny.

" Perhaps he shut it behind him," said Murphy.

They returned to the foot of the ladder.

" A million thanks," said Murphy.

" Well, that beats everything," said Ticklepenny.

Murphy tried to pull the ladder up after him. It was fastened down.

" Come on down to the club for a bit," said Ticklepenny, " why don't you ? "

Murphy closed the trap.

" Well, that beats the band," said Ticklepenny, shambling away.

Murphy moved the radiator as close to the bed as it would reach, sagged willingly in the middle according to the mattress and tried to come out in his mind. His body being too active with its fatigue to permit of this, he submitted to sleep, Sleep son of Erebus and Night, Sleep half-brother to the Furies.

When he awoke the fug was thick. He got up and opened the skylight to see what stars he commanded, but closed it again at once, there being no stars. He lit the tall thick candle from the radiator and went down to the w.c. to shut off the flow. What was the etymology of gas? On his way back he examined the foot of the ladder. It was only lightly screwed down, Ticklepenny could rectify it. He undressed to the regulation shirt, stuck the candle by its own tallow to the floor at the head of the bed, got in and tried to come out in his mind. But his body was still too busy with its fatigue. And the etymology of gas? Could it be the same word as chaos? Hardly. Chaos was yawn. But then cretin was Christian. Chaos would do, it might not be right but it was pleasant, for him henceforward gas would be chaos, and chaos gas. It could make you yawn, warm, laugh, cry, cease to suffer, live a little longer, die a little sooner. What could it not do? Gas. Could it turn a neurotic into a psychotic? No. Only

God could do that. Let there be Heaven in the midst of the waters, let it divide the waters from the waters. The Chaos and Waters Facilities Act. The Chaos, Light and Coke Co. Hell. Heaven. Helen. Celia.

In the morning nothing remained of the dream but a postmonition of calamity, nothing of the candle but a little coil of tallow.

Nothing remained but to see what he wanted to see. Any fool can turn the blind eye, but who knows what the ostrich sees in the sand?

He would not have admitted that he needed a brotherhood. He did. In the presence of this issue (psychiatric-psychotic) between the life from which he had turned away and the life of which he had no experience, except as he hoped inchoately in himself, he could not fail to side with the latter. His first impressions (always the best), hope of better things, feeling of kindred, etc., had been in that sense. Nothing remained but to substantiate these, distorting all that threatened to belie them. It was strenuous work, but very pleasant.

Thus it was necessary that every hour in the wards should increase, together with his esteem for the patients, his loathing of the text-book attitude towards them, the complacent scientific conceptualism that made contact with outer reality the index of mental well-being. Every hour did.

The nature of outer reality remained obscure. The men, women and children of science would seem to have as many ways of kneeling to their facts as any other body of illuminati. The definition of outer reality, or of reality short and simple, varied according to the sensibility of the definer. But all seemed agreed that contact with it, even the layman's muzzy contact, was a rare privilege.

On this basis the patients were described as " cut off " from reality, from the rudimentary blessings of the layman's reality, if not altogether, as in the severer cases, then in certain fundamental respects. The function of treatment was to bridge the gulf, translate the sufferer from his own pernicious little private dungheap to the glorious world of discrete particles, where it would be his inestimable prerogative once again to wonder, love, hate, desire, rejoice and howl in a reasonable balanced manner, and comfort himself with the society of others in the same predicament.

All this was duly revolting to Murphy, whose experience as a physical and rational being obliged him to call sanctuary what the psychi-

atrists called exile and to think of the patients
not as banished from a system of benefits but
as escaped from a colossal fiasco. If his mind
had been on the correct cash-register lines,
an indefatigable apparatus for doing sums with
the petty cash of current facts, then no doubt
the suppression of these would have seemed
a deprivation. But since it was not, since
what he called his mind functioned not as an
instrument but as a place, from whose unique
delights precisely those current facts withheld
him, was it not most natural that he should
welcome their suppression, as of gyves?

The issue therefore, as lovingly simplified and
perverted by Murphy, lay between nothing less
fundamental than the big world and the little
world, decided by the patients in favour of
the latter, revived by the psychiatrists on behalf
of the former, in his own case unresolved. In
fact, it was unresolved, only in fact. His vote
was cast. " I am not of the big world, I am
of the little world " was an old refrain with
Murphy, and a conviction, two convictions,
the negative first. How should he tolerate,
let alone cultivate, the occasions of fiasco, having
once beheld the beatific idols of his cave?
In the beautiful Belgo-Latin of Arnold Geulincx :
Ubi nihil vales, ibi nihil velis.

But it was not enough to want nothing where he was worth nothing, nor even to take the further step of renouncing all that lay outside the intellectual love in which alone he could love himself, because there alone he was lovable. It had not been enough and showed no signs of being enough. These dispositions and others ancillary, pressing every available means (e.g. the rocking-chair) into their service, could sway the issue in the desired direction, but not clinch it. It continued to divide him, as witness his deplorable susceptibility to Celia, ginger, and so on. The means of clinching it were lacking. Suppose he were to clinch it now, in the service of the Clinch clan! That would indeed be very pretty.

The frequent expressions apparently of pain, rage, despair and in fact all the usual, to which some patients gave vent, suggesting a fly somewhere in the ointment of Microcosmos, Murphy either disregarded or muted to mean what he wanted. Because these outbursts presented more or less the same features as those current in Mayfair and Clapham, it did not follow that they were identically provoked, any more than it was possible to argue the livers of those areas from the gloomy panoply of melancholia. But even if the Eton and Waterloo causes could be established behind these simulacra of their

effects, even if the patients did sometimes feel
as lousy as they sometimes looked, still no
aspersion was necessarily cast on the little world
where Murphy presupposed them, one and all,
to be having a glorious time. One had merely
to ascribe their agitations, not to any flaw
in their self-seclusion, but to its investment by
the healers. The melancholic's melancholy, the
manic's fits of fury, the paranoid's despair, were
no doubt as little autonomous as the long fat
face of a mute. Left in peace they would have
been as happy as Larry, short for Lazarus,
whose raising seemed to Murphy perhaps the one
occasion on which the Messiah had overstepped
the mark.

With these and even less weighty constructions
he saved his facts against the pressure of those
current in the Mercyseat. Stimulated by all
those lives immured in mind, as he insisted on
supposing, he laboured more diligently than
ever before at his own little dungeon in Spain.
Three factors especially encouraged him in
this and in the belief that he had found his
kindred at last. The first was the absolute
impassiveness of the higher schizoids, in the
face of the most pitiless therapeutic bombard-
ment. The second was the padded cells. The
third was his success with the patients.

The first of these, after what has been said of Murphy's own bondage, speaks for itself. What more vigorous fillip could be given to the wallows of one bogged in the big world than the example of life to all appearances inalienably realised in the little ?

The pads surpassed by far all he had even been able to imagine in the way of indoor bowers of bliss. The three dimensions, slightly concave, were so exquisitely proportioned that the absence of the fourth was scarcely felt. The tender luminous oyster-grey of the pneumatic upholstery, cushioning every square inch of ceiling, walls, floor and door, lent colour to the truth, that one was a prisoner of air. The temperature was such that only total nudity could do it justice. No system of ventilation appeared to dispel the illusion of respirable vacuum. The compartment was windowless, like a monad, except for the shuttered judas in the door, at which a sane eye appeared, or was employed to appear, at frequent and regular intervals throughout the twenty-four hours. Within the narrow limits of domestic architecture he had never been able to imagine a more creditable representation of what he kept on calling, indefatigably, the little world.

His success with the patients was little short

of scandalous. According to the text-book psychotic, with his tendency to equate those objects, ideas, persons, etc., evincing the least element in common, the patients should have identified Murphy with Bom & Co., simply because he resembled them in the superficial matters of function and clothing. The great majority failed to do so. The great majority discriminated so unmistakably in Murphy's favour that even Bom lost a little of his high colour. Whatever they were in the habit of doing for Bom & Co., they did more readily for Murphy. And in certain matters where Bom & Co. were obliged to coerce them, or restrain them, they would suffer Murphy to persuade them. One patient, a litigious case of doubtful category, refused to exercise unless accompanied by Murphy. Another, a melancholic with highly developed delusions of guilt, would not get out of his bed unless on Murphy's invitation. Another melancholic, convinced that his intestines had turned to twine and blotting-paper, would only eat when Murphy held the spoon. Otherwise he had to be force-fed. All this was highly irregular, little short of scandalous.

Murphy was revolted by Suk's attribution of this strange talent solely to the moon in the Serpent at the hour of his birth. The more his own system closed round him, the less he could tolerate its being subordinated to any other. Between him and his stars no doubt there was correspondence, but not in Suk's sense. They were *his* stars, he was the prior system. He had been projected, larval and dark, on the sky of that regrettable hour as on a screen, magnified and clarified into his own meaning. But it was *his* meaning. The moon in the Serpent was no more than an image, a fragment of vitagraph.

Thus the sixpence worth of sky changed again, from the poem that he alone of all the living could write to the poem that he alone of all the born could have written. So far as the prophetic status of the celestial bodies was concerned Murphy had become an out-and-out preterist.

Free therefore to inspect for the first time *in situ* that " great magical ability of the eye to which the lunatic would easy succumb ", Murphy was gratified to find how well it consisted with what he knew already of his idiosyncrasy. His success with the patients· was the signpost at last on the way he had followed so long and so blindly, with nothing to sustain him but the conviction that all other ways were wrong. His success with the patients was a signpost pointing to them. It meant that they felt in him what they had been and he in them what he would be. It meant that nothing less than a slap-up psychosis could consummate his life's strike. *Quod erat extorquendum.*

It seemed to Murphy that of all his friends among the patients there was none quite like his " tab ", Mr. Endon his " tab ". It seemed to Murphy that he was bound to Mr. Endon, not by the tab only, but by a love of the purest possible kind, exempt from the big world's precocious ejaculations of thought, word and deed. They remained to one another, even when most profoundly one in spirit, as it seemed to Murphy, Mr. Murphy and Mr. Endon.

A " tab " was a patient " on parchment " (or " on caution "). A patient was put on parchment (or on caution) whenever there was occasion to suspect him of serious suicidal leanings. The occasion might be threats uttered by the patient or it might be simply the general tenor of his behaviour. Then a tab was issued in his name, specifying in all cases where a preference had been expressed the form of suicide contemplated. Thus : " Mr. Higgins. The bellycut, or any other available means." " Mr. O'Connor. Venom, or any other available means." " Any other available means " was a saving clause. The tab was then passed on to the male sister, who having endorsed it passed it on to one of his male nurses, who having endorsed it was from that time forward responsible for the natural death of the bastard in question. Of the special duties entailed by this responsibility, perhaps the chief was the control of the suspect at regular intervals of not more than twenty minutes. For it was the experience of the Mercyseat that only the most skilful and determined could do the trick in less time than that.

Mr. Endon was on parchment and Murphy had his tab : " Mr. Endon. Apnœa, or any other available means."

Suicide by apnœa has often been tried, notably by the condemned to death. In vain. It is a physiological impossibility. But the Mercyseat was not disposed to take unnecessary chances. Mr. Endon had insisted that if he did it at all, it would be by apnœa, and not otherwise. He said his voice would not hear of any other method. But Dr. Killiecrankie, the Outer Hebridean R.M.S., had some experience of the schizoid voice. It was not like a real voice, one minute it said one thing and the next minute something quite different. Nor was he entirely satisfied as to the physiological impossibility of suicide by apnœa. Dr.

Killiecrankie had been too often had by the resources of organic matter ever again to draw the Canutian line.

Mr. Endon was a schizophrenic of the most amiable variety, at least for the purposes of such a humble and envious outsider as Murphy. The languor in which he passed his days, while deepening every now and then to the extent of some charming suspension of gesture, was never so profound as to inhibit all movement. His inner voice did not harangue him, it was unobtrusive and melodious, a gentle continuo in the whole consort of his hallucinations. The bizarrerie of his attitudes never exceeded a stress laid on their grace. In short, a psychosis so limpid and imperturbable that Murphy felt drawn to it as Narcissus to his fountain.

The tiny body was perfect in every detail and extremely hairy. The features were most delicate, regular and winning, the complexion olive except where blue with beard. The skull, large for any body, immense for this, crackled with stiff black hair broken at the crown by one wide tress of bright white. Mr. Endon did not dress, but drifted about the wards in a fine dressing-gown of scarlet byssus faced with black braid, black silk pyjamas and neo-merovingian poulaines of deepest purple. His fingers blazed with rings. He held tight in his little fist the butt, varying in length according to the hour, of an excellent cigar. This Murphy would light for him in the morning and keep on lighting throughout the day. Yet evening found it still unfinished.

It was the same with chess, Mr. Endon's one frivolity. Murphy would set up the game, as soon as he came on in the morning, in a quiet corner of the wreck, make his move (for he always played white), go away, come back to Mr. Endon's reply, make his second move, go away, and so on throughout the day. They came together at the board but seldom. One or two minutes was as long as Mr. Endon cared to pause in his drifting, longer than Murphy dared snatch from his duties and the vigilance of Bom. Each made his move in the absence of the other, inspected the position with what time remained, and went away. So the game wore on, till evening found it almost as level as when begun. This was due not so much to their being evenly matched, or to the unfavourable conditions of play, as to the very Fabian methods that both adopted. How little the issue was really engaged may be judged from the fact that sometimes, after eight or nine hours of this guerrilla, neither player

would have lost a piece or even checked the
other. This pleased Murphy as an expression
of his kinship with Mr. Endon and made him
if possible more chary of launching an attack
than by nature he was.

He was sorry for himself, very sorry, when
eight o'clock came and he had to leave the wards,
Mr. Endon and the lesser friends and exemplars,
the warmth and smell of peraldehyde, etc., to
face the twelve hours of self, unredeemed split
self, now more than ever the best he could do
and less than ever good enough. The end
degrades the way into a means, a sceneless tedium.
Yet he had to welcome the inkling of the end.

The garret, the fug, sleep, these were the poor
best he could do. Ticklepenny had unscrewed
the ladder, so that now he could draw it up
after him. Do not come down the ladder,
they have taken it away.

He did not see the stars any more. Walking
back from Skinner's his eyes were on the ground.
And when it was not too cold to open the skylight in the garret, the stars seemed always
veiled by cloud or fog or mist. The sad truth
was that the skylight commanded only that
most dismal patch of night sky, the galactic
coal-sack, which would naturally look like a
dirty night to any observer in Murphy's condi-

tion, cold, tired, angry, impatient and out of conceit with a system that seemed the superfluous cartoon of his own.

Nor did he think of Celia any more, though he could sometimes remember having dreamt of her. If only he had been able to think of her, he would not have needed to dream of her.

Nor did he succeed in coming alive in his mind any more. He blamed this on his body, fussy with its fatigue after so much duty, but it was rather due to the vicarious autology that he had been enjoying since morning, in little Mr. Endon and all the other proxies. That was why he felt happy in the wards and sorry when the time came to leave them. He could not have it both ways, not even the illusion of it.

He thought of the rocking-chair left behind in Brewery Road, that aid to life in his mind from which he had never before been parted. His books, his pictures, his postcards, his musical scores and instruments, all had been gradually disposed of in that order rather than the chair. He worried about it more and more as the week of day duty drew to an end and the week of night duty approached.

The garret, the fug, fatigue, night, the hours of vicarious autology, these had made it possible

for him to do without the chair. But night
duty would be different. Then there would
be no appeasement by proxy, for Mr. Endon
and his kind would be sleeping. Then there
would be no fatigue, for watching could not
fatigue him. But he would find himself in the
morning, with all the hours of light before him,
hungry in mind, docile in body, craving for
the chair.

Saturday was his afternoon off and he hastened
to Brewery Road. In a way, the one way,
the immemorial way, he was sorry to find Celia
out. In all other ways, glad. For whether
he answered her questions or not, told the truth
or lied, she would know that he was gone. He
did not want her to feel, at least he did not
want to be present when she felt, how far all
her loving nagging had gone astray ; how it
had only served to set him up more firmly than
before in the position against which it had been
trained, the position in which she had found
him and would not leave him ; how her efforts
to make a man of him had made him more
than ever Murphy ; and how by insisting on
trying to change him she had lost him, as he
had warned her she would. " You, my body,
my mind . . . one must go."

It was night when he reached the garret with

the chair, having satisfied himself on the way up that no one was about, least of all in the w.c. Almost at once gas, reminding him that he had forgotten to turn it on, began to pour through the radiator. This could not alarm him, who was not tied by interest to a corpse-obedient matter and whose best friends had always been among things. He merely felt greatly obliged, that he had not to let down the ladder and go and repair his omission.

He lit the radiator, undressed, got into the chair but did not tie himself up. Gently does these things, sit down before you lie down. When he came to, or rather from, how he had no idea, the first thing he saw was the fug, the next sweat on his thigh, the next Ticklepenny as though thrown on the silent screen by Griffith in midshot soft-focus sprawling on the bed, suggesting how he might have been roused.

" I lit the candle," said Ticklepenny, " the better to marvel at you."

Murphy did not move, any more than one does for an animal, or an animal for one. The instinctive curiosities also, as to how long Ticklepenny had been there, what he wanted at that dead hour, how he had contrived to intrude with the ladder removed, etc., were too indolent to discharge in words.

" I could not sleep," said Ticklepenny. " You are the only pal I have in this kip. I called and called. I threw my handball against the trap, again and again, with all my might. I got the wind up. I ran and got my little steps."

" I suppose if I had a lock put on the trap," said Murphy, " my pals would come in through the skylight."

" You fascinate me," said Ticklepenny, " fast asleep in the dark with your eyes wide open, like an owl is it not? "

" I was not asleep," said Murphy.

" Oh," said Ticklepenny, " then you did hear me."

Murphy looked at Ticklepenny.

" Oh," said Ticklepenny, " just deep in thought then or plunged in a reverie maybe."

" What do you take me for ? " said Murphy. " The student of my year ? "

" Then what ? " said Ticklepenny. " If it is not a rude question."

Murphy amused himself bitterly and briefly with the question of the answer he would have made to a person of his own steak and kidney, genuinely anxious to understand and desirable of being understood by, a Mr. Endon at his own degree of incipience for example. But

before the imperfect phrase had time to come
the question crumbled away in its own absurdity,
the absurdity of saddling such a person with
the rationalist prurit, the sceptic rut that places
the objects of its curiosity on the level of Les
Girls. It was not under that the rare birds of
Murphy's feather desired to stand, but by, by
themselves with the best of their attention and
by the others of their species with any that might
be left over. It was not in order to obtain
an obscene view of the surface that in days
gone by the Great Auk dived under the ice,
the Great Auk now no longer seen above it.

" I do not know exactly what you want,"
said Murphy, " but I can tell you there is
nothing I can do for you that would not be
done better by anyone else. So why stay ? "

" Do you know what it is ? " said Ticklepenny,
" no offence meant, you had a great look of
Clarke there a minute ago."

Clarke had been for three weeks in a katatonic
stupor.

" All but the cackle," said Ticklepenny.

Clarke would repeat for hours the phrase :
" Mr. Endon is *very* superior."

The gratified look that Murphy disdained to
hide so alarmed Ticklepenny that he abandoned
his purpose and rose to go, just as Murphy

would not have objected to his staying a little
longer. He lowered himself over the threshold,
he stood on his steps with only his head appearing. He said :

" You want to watch yourself."

" In what way ? " said Murphy.

" You want to mind your health," said
Ticklepenny.

" In what way did I remind you of Clarke ? "
said Murphy.

" You want to take a pull on yourself," said
Ticklepenny. " Good night."

And in effect Murphy's night was good,
perhaps the best since nights began so long
ago to be bad, the reason being not so much that
he had his chair again as that the self whom
he loved had the aspect, even to Ticklepenny's
inexpert eye, of a real alienation. Or to put
it perhaps more nicely : conferred that aspect
on the self whom he hated.

10

Miss Counihan and Wylie were not living together !

The decaying Haydn, invited to give his opinion of cohabitation, replied : " Parallel thirds." But the partition of Miss Counihan and Wylie had more concrete grounds.

To begin with Miss Counihan, to begin with she was eager to get into the correct grass Dido cramp in plenty of time. She did not want to leave it to the last moment, until they were actually haling Murphy before her, and then have to scour London for a pyre that was clean, comfortable, central and not exorbitant. So she found without delay, and imparted in block capitals to Wylie, an address in Gower Street where she was on no account to be disturbed. It was almost opposite the offices of the *Spectator*, but she did not discover this until it was too late. Here she cowered, as happy as the night was short, in the midst of Indians, Egyptians, Cyprians, Japanese, Chinese, Siamese

and clergymen. Little by little she sucked up
to a Hindu polyhistor of dubious caste. He had
been writing for many years, still was and trusted
he would be granted Prana to finish, a mono-
graph provisionally entitled : *The Pathetic Fallacy
from Avercamp to Kampendonck*. But already he
began to complain of those sensations that some
weeks later, just as he stumbled on the Norwich
School for the first time, were to drive him
to the gas-oven. " My fut," he had said to
Miss Counihan, " 'ave gut smaller than the
end of the needle." And again : " I want to
be up in the air."

Then Miss Counihan had to be free to twist
Wylie and this was perhaps her best reason for
keeping him at a distance. She bribed and
browbeat Cooper into reporting to her at the
end of every day before he did so to Wylie ;
and directed by Cooper she went to Neary behind
Wylie's back and made a clean breast of the
whole situation.

Wylie protested bitterly against this cruel
treatment, which suited him down to the muck.
For Miss Counihan was not one of those delights
peculiar to London, with which he proposed
to indulge himself up to the hilt and the utmost
limit of her liberality. It was only in Dublin,
where the profession had gone to the dogs, that

Miss Counihan could stand out as the object of desire of a man of taste. If Neary had not been cured of her by London, he was less than a man, or more than a saint. Turf is compulsory in the Saorstat, but one need not bring a private supply to Newcastle.

His other reason for satisfaction with the turn events had taken, or been so kindly given by Miss Counihan, was of course the same as hers, namely, that he could now double-cross her in perfect comfort and security. He browbeat Cooper (but did not bribe him) into reporting to him at the end of every day before he did so to Miss Counihan; and directed by Cooper he went to Neary behind Miss Counihan's back and made a clean breast of the whole situation that was the complement of hers.

Such were the chief grounds for the partition, which was not however so inflexible that they could not contrive, now and then after supper, to meet on neutral ground and compare notes and ruts.

Cooper experienced none of the famous difficulty in serving two employers. He neither clave nor despised. A lesser man would have sided with one or the other, a bigger blackmailed both. But Cooper was the perfect size

for the servant so long as he kept off the bottle
and he moved incorruptible between his
corruptors with the beautiful indifference of
a shuttle, without infamy and without praise.
To each he made a full and frank report,
ignoring the emendations of the other ; and
made it first to whichever of the two was more
convenient to the point at which dusk surprised
him.

He did not try to reinstate himself with Neary,
feeling it might be wiser to wait till Neary sent
for him. He also felt a shade less wretched
as the coadjutor of a pair of twisters, who not
only knew next to nothing about him but seemed
in a fair way to being as crapulous as himself,
than as the catspaw of a hardened toff, who
knew all, including much that he himself had
contrived to forget. Did it perhaps mark the
beginning, this slight loss of misery, of that
fuller life that Wylie had dangled before him
in Dublin? " In a short time you will be sitting
down and taking off your hat and doing all
the things that are impossible at present. . . ."
Cooper thought it unlikely.

The relief to Neary was so great that he
relaxed and went to bed, vowing not to get up
till news of Murphy should be brought to him.
He wrote to Miss Counihan :

" I can never forget your loyalty. One person at least I can trust. Keep Judas Wylie on your hands. Tell Cooper he serves me in serving you. Come when you have news of Murphy, not before. It is too painful. Then you shall not find me ungrateful."

And to Wylie :

" I can never forget your loyalty. You at least will not betray me. Tell Cooper your favour is mine. Keep Jezabel Counihan on your hands. Come again when Murphy is found, not before. It is too trying. Then you shall find me not ungrateful."

Neary was indeed cured of Miss Counihan, as completely and finally as though she had bowed, in the manner of Miss Dwyer, to his wishes ; but by means very different from those to which Wylie had responded so splendidly. In Wylie's case, properly speaking, it was less a matter of cure than of convalescence. For Miss Counihan had already been bowing, or rather nodding, to his wishes, or rather whims, for long enough to make further homeopathy unnecessary.

It is curious how Wylie's words remained fixed in the minds of those to whom they had once been addressed. It must have been the tone of voice. Cooper, whose memory for such things was really very poor, had recovered, word for word, the merest of mere phrases. And now Neary lay on his bed, repeating : "The syndrome known as life is too diffuse to admit of palliation. For every symptom that is eased, another is made worse. The horse leech's daughter is a closed system. Her quantum of wantum cannot vary."

He thought of his latest *voltefesses*, at once so pleasant and so painful. Pleasant, in that Miss Counihan had been eased ; painful, in that Murphy had been made worse ; *fesses*, as being the part best qualified by nature not only to be kicked but also to mock the kicker, a paradox strikingly illustrated by Socrates, when he turned up the tail of his abolla at the trees.

Was his need any less for the sudden transformation of Murphy from the key that would open Miss Counihan to the one and only earthly hope of friendship and all that friendship carried with it ? (Neary's conception of friendship was very curious. He expected it to last. He never said, when speaking of an enemy : "He used to be a friend of mine ", but always, with affected precision : "I used to think he was a friend of mine.") Was his need any less ? It felt greater, but might well be the same. "The advantage of this view is, that while one may not look forward to things getting any better, at least one need not fear their getting any worse. They will always be the same as they always were."

He writhed on his back in the bed, yearning for Murphy as though he had never yearned for anything or anyone before. He turned over and buried his face in the pillow, folding up its wings till they met at the back of his neck, and could not but remark how pleasant it was to feel for a change the weight of his bottom on his belly after so many hours of the converse distribution. But keeping his head resolutely buried and enveloped he groaned : " *Le pou est mort. Vive le pou !* " And a little later, being by then almost stifled : " Is there no flea that found at last dies without issue ? No keyflea ? "

It was from just this consideration that Murphy, while still less than a child, had set out to capture himself, not with anger but with love. This was a stroke of genius that Neary, a Newtonian, could never have dealt himself nor suffered another to deal him. There seems really very little hope for Neary, he seems doomed to hope unending. He has something of Hugo. The fire will not depart from his eye, nor the

water from his mouth, as he scratches himself
out of one itch into the next, until he shed his
mortal mange, supposing that to be permitted.

Murphy then is actually being needed by
five people outside himself. By Celia, because
she loves him. By Neary, because he thinks
of him as the Friend at last. By Miss Counihan,
because she wants a surgeon. By Cooper,
because he is being employed to that end. By
Wylie, because he is reconciled to doing Miss
Counihan the honour, in the not too distant
future, of becoming her husband. Not only
did she stand out in Dublin and in Cork as quite
exceptionally anthropoid, but she had private
means.

Note that of all these reasons love alone
did not splutter towards its end. Not because
it was Love, but because there were no means
at its disposal. When its end had been Murphy
transfigured and transformed, happily caught
up in some salaried routine, means had not
been lacking. Now that its end was Murphy
at any price, in whatsoever shape or form, so
long as he was lovable, i.e. present in person,
means were lacking, as Murphy had warned
her they would be. Women are really extraordinary, the way they want to give their cake
to the cat and have it. They never quite kill

the thing they think they love, lest their instinct for artificial respiration should go abegging.

As Gower Street was more convenient to Brewery Road than was Earl's Court, where Wylie had found a sitting-bedroom, it was to Miss Counihan that Cooper first hastened with the news that Murphy's woman had been run to earth at last, and the astute comment that where a man's woman was, there it was only a question of time before that man would be also.

"Who says she is his woman?" hissed Miss Counihan. "Describe the bitch."

Cooper with sure instinct took refuge in the dusk, the suspense, the distance he had had to keep, the posterior aspect (surely a very thin excuse), and so on. For of the infinite criticisms of Murphy's woman that could have been devised, from loathing to enthusiasm, there was not one but must have caused Miss Counihan pain. Because either a drab had been preferred to her, or else a woman more exquisite than herself existed, either of which was a proposition too painful to be borne in the mouth of a man, even though that man were only Cooper.

"Not a word to a soul," said Miss Counihan. "What number again in Brewery Road did you say ? Remember it has been just another blank day. Here is a florin I believe."

She unpinned and unbuttoned herself as she spoke. Clearly she was in a great hurry to get off her things. She never reflected, to give her her due, that Cooper for all his shortcomings was a man like other men, with passions just like theirs, namely made to fit hers.

" And to-morrow," she said, stepping out of her step-ins, " you set off in the morning as usual, but not to look for Murphy—here, damn it, I will make it half a crown—but to look for Mrs. Neary. Mrs. Neary," she repeated an octave higher, " Ariadne bloody Neary, misbegotten Cox, more pippin than orange no doubt, though personally," with a sigh and milder voice snapping open her corset, " I have nothing against the poor wretch, unless you hear to the contrary."

The interview with Wylie was less trying to Cooper, and less lucrative, for Wylie was at the end of his resources, until he should see Miss Counihan again.

Wylie's mind belonged to the same great group as Miss Counihan's.

" Drop Murphy," he said, " forget him and get after the Cox."

Cooper waited for the rest, but Wylie put on his hat and coat, said, " After you, Cooper ", then not another word till in the street, " How do you go now, Cooper?"

Cooper had not given this a thought. He indicated a direction at a venture.

" Then I'll be saying good night, Cooper," said Wylie. But after a few paces he pulled up with the air of one who suddenly remembers, stood stock still for a second and then turned back to where Cooper, neither impatient nor amused, was waiting.

" I nearly forgot to say," he said, " that when you see Miss Counihan—you will be seeing her now, won't you, Cooper?"

The skill is really extraordinary with which analphabetes, especially those of Irish education, circumvent their dread of verbal commitments. Now Cooper's face, though it did not seem to move a muscle, brought together and threw off in a single grimace the finest shades of irresolution, revulsion, doglike devotion, catlike discretion, fatigue, hunger, thirst and reserves of strength, in a very small fraction of the time that the finest oratory would require for a greatly inferior evasion, and without exposing its proprietor to misquotation.

" Don't I know," said Wylie. " But just in case you should, remember there is nothing new, not a thing to report. You know what women are when it comes to women."

If Cooper did not possess this knowledge it was not for lack of an occasion, a melancholy occasion, of which perhaps the most regrettable result was this, that of the only two good angels he had ever been able to care for, simultaneously as ill luck would have it, the one, a Miss A, then a brunette, was now in her seventeenth year of His Majesty's pleasure, while the other, a Miss B, also formerly a brunette, had not yet succumbed to her injuries. Yet properly speaking the knowledge was not his, it was not present to him as an everyday precaution as it was to Wylie, and to Neary, and indeed to most men, though they gain it at far less cost, and even in some cases *a priori*. For the bitter blow was one of those referred to above, forgotten almost entirely at great pains by Cooper and at scarcely less pains almost in its entirety re-constructed by Neary. What the former could still recall, because it did not pain him, and the latter had never known, because it did not interest him, was the merest scene of tenderness or two, with Miss A before he met Miss B, and again with Miss B before she met Miss A.

" I say you know what women are," said Wylie impatiently, " or has your entire life been spent in Cork ? "

Cooper's head toppled forward and his hands,

small, white, numb, sodden, hairless, but actually
quite dexterous, toiled up a little through the
dark. He said :

" That'll be all right."

" Or is there perhaps some fair charmer,"
said Wylie, " that blinds you to her sex ? Some
young person ? Come now, Cooper."

Cooper dropped his hands, forced his head
round to look at Wylie and said, in much
the same dead tone :

" That will be all right."

Night had scarcely fallen and yet already
Neary, his pyjamas torn from his body and
flung on the floor, was tossing under a sheet,
wondering would morning never come, when
Miss Counihan was announced. Seeing that
he was not disposed to get up and make much
of her, she seated herself with a desinvolture
she was far from feeling on the end of the bed,
as though it were a bank of bluebells somewhere
in the country. Under the sheet his icy feet
were crossed and crispated like talons on a hot-
water bag. For it tickled his smattering of
Greek urns, where Sleep was figured with crossed
feet, and frequently also Sleep's young brother,
to cross his whenever he felt wakeful. Also he
had some vague theory about his terminals

being thereby connected, and his life force prevented from escaping. But now with sleep out of the question, and Miss Counihan's hot buttered buttocks so close, he uncrossed his feet and kicked the bag out of the bed, on the wall side. It burst on the floor without a sound, so that water is oozing towards the centre of the floor throughout the scene that follows.

In a somewhat similar way Celia had sat on Mr. Kelly's bed, and on Murphy's, though Mr. Kelly had had his shirt on.

They had not been closeted together very long and Miss Counihan, choking with mortification, had not yet succeeded in persuading Neary that who found Celia found Murphy also, when Wylie was announced. Miss Counihan shot off the bed and cast round wildly for a way of escape or a place of concealment.

"Curtains collect the dirt so," said Neary, "that I never have them. I fear you would not pass through the door of my cupboard, not even sideways, not even frontways rather. There is no balcony. I hesitate to suggest under the bed."

Miss Counihan flew to the door, locked it and took out the key, even as Wylie knocked.

"I am sorry there is no staple to put your arm through," said Neary.

Wylie tore at the handle, calling, " It is I,
it is Needle." Miss Counihan threw herself
on Neary's mercy, not by word of mouth obviously, but with bended knee, panting bosom,
clasped hands, passion-dimmed belladonna, etc.

" Come in," cried Neary. " Miss Counihan
has locked you out."

Miss Counihan rose from the floor.

" If your tart will not let you in," cried Neary,
" stay where you are, I have rung for the
chamber pot."

But Miss Counihan did not know when she
was beaten, or, if she did, her way of showing
it was unusual. For it did not require a
woman of her resource and experience to go
off into peals of mischievous laughter, fling
open the door and pass the whole thing off
as a joke. Instead she sat down quietly in a
chair and waited for the chambermaid to come
and let Wylie in. She must have preferred,
all things rapidly considered, the few moments
thus snatched from the show-down, in which
to revise her strategy, to a cut-and-dried tactic
affording only temporary relief. No, Miss Counihan did not know when she was beaten.

There was now the usual calm after storm,
Neary sitting up in the bed and feasting his eyes
on Miss Counihan, Miss Counihan absorbed

in her problem tapping her teeth thought-
fully with the key, Wylie on the other side of
the door exactly half inclined to tiptoe away,
the chambermaid far away in her dark cavern
waiting for the bell to ring a second time.
When it did, proving with a single peal that
the summons was seriously intended and that
her hearing had not deceived her, she set off
without rancour and in a short time was knocking
at the door.

"The gentleman is locked out," called Neary.
"Let him in."

Wylie strode in much too boldly and Miss
Counihan rose.

"Good girl," said Neary. "Now lock the
door behind the gentleman."

Wylie and Miss Counihan met face to face,
a trying experience for them both.

"You cur," said Miss Counihan, getting her
blow in first.

"You bitch," said Wylie.

They belonged to the same great group.

"You take the tone out of my mouth," said
Neary, "if not the terms."

"You cur," said Miss Counihan, making a
bid for the last word.

"Before you go any further——" said Neary.

The first round was Miss Counihan's and her

forces were still intact. She sat down and Wylie
moved over to the bed. He was equipped by
nature to feel a situation, and adjust himself
to it, more rapidly than Miss Counihan, but
she had the advantage of a short start.

" This lock-out," said Neary, " don't misunderstand it whatever you do."

" I think more highly of you than that," said
Wylie.

" *I* thank you," said Neary, like a London
bus or tram conductor tendered the exact fare.

It struck Miss Counihan with sudden force
that here were two men, against whom she
could never prevail, even were her cause a just
one.

" And no doubt your great piece of news
is the same as your doxy's," said Neary, " that
Cooper has picked up a woman with whom a
glimpse of Murphy was once caught."

" She was not exactly seen with him," said
Wylie, " only entering the house where he was
known to be at that time."

" And you call this finding Murphy," said
Neary.

" Cooper feels it in his bones," said Wylie,
" and so do I, that this beautiful woman will
lead us to him."

" Uric acid," said Neary.

" But if Miss Counihan believes," said Wylie, " who are we to doubt ? "

Miss Counihan bit her lip that she had not thought of this argument, which opened and closed Neary's mouth a number of times. He found it forcible—and he craved to get up.

" If you, Wylie," he said, " will pass me up my pyjamas, and you, Miss Counihan, take notice that I shall emerge from under this sheet incomparably more naked than the day I was born, I shall break my bed." Wylie passed up the pyjamas and Miss Counihan covered her eyes. " Do not be alarmed, Wylie," said Neary, " the vast majority are bedsores." He sat on the edge of the bed in his pyjamas. " It is no use my trying to stand," he said, " nothing is more exhausting than a long rest in bed, so now, Miss Counihan, when you like."

Miss Counihan stole a look and was so far moved from her grievances as to say :

" Surely we could make you a little more comfortable ? "

Here the keyword was we, a little finger of reconciliation extended to Wylie. Without it the phrase was merely polite, or, at the best, kind. It did not escape Wylie, who looked most willing to be helpful all over.

From the moment that Neary, breaking his

bed, admitted that Murphy was found, from the moment namely that on this one point at least they were agreed not to differ, a notable change for the better had come over the atmosphere, now one almost of reciprocal tolerance.

" Nothing can surprise me any more," said Neary.

Miss Counihan and Wylie sprang forward, worked Neary on to his feet, supported him to a chair in the window, lowered him into it.

" The whiskey is under the bed," said Neary.

It was at this moment that they all saw simultaneously for the first time, and with common good breeding refrained from remarking, the slender meanders of water on the floor. Miss Counihan however would not have any whiskey. Wylie raised his glass and said : " To the absentee ", a tactful description of Murphy under the circumstances. Miss Counihan honoured this toast with a strong intake of breath.

" Sit down, the two of you, there before me," said Neary, " and do not despair. Remember there is no triangle, however obtuse, but the circumference of some circle passes through its wretched vertices. Remember also one thief was saved."

" Our medians," said Wylie, " or whatever the hell they are, meet in Murphy."

" Outside us," said Neary. " Outside us."

" In the outer light," said Miss Counihan.
Now it was Wylie's turn, but he could find
nothing. No sooner did he realise this, that
he would not find anything in time to do himself
credit, than he began to look as though he were
not looking for anything, nay, as though he
were waiting for it to be his turn. Finally
Neary said without pity :

" You to play, Needle."

" And do the lady out of the last word ! "
cried Wylie. " And put the lady to the trouble
of finding another ! Reary, Neally ! "

" No trouble," said Miss Counihan.

Now it was anybody's turn.

" Very well," said Neary. " What I was
really coming to, what I wanted to suggest,
is this. Let our conversation now be without
precedent in fact or literature, each one speaking
to the best of his ability the truth to the best
of his knowledge. That is what I meant when
I said you took the tone, if not the terms, out
of my mouth. It is high time we three parted."

" But the tone was bitter, I believe," said
Wylie. " That certainly was my impression."

" I was not thinking of the tone of voice,"
said Neary, " so much as of the tone of
mind, the spirit's approach. But continue,

Wylie, by all means. Might not the truth be snarled ? "

" Coleridge-Taylor played with feeling ? " said Wylie.

" A perfume thrown on the horehound ? " said Miss Counihan.

" The guillotine sterilised ? " said Wylie.

" Floodlit the midnight sun ? " said Miss Counihan.

" We look on the dark side," said Neary. " It is undeniably less trying to the eyes."

" What you suggest is abominable," said Wylie, " an insult to human nature."

" Not at all," said Neary. " Listen to this."

" I must be off," said Miss Counihan.

Neary began to speak, or, as it rather sounded, be spoken through. For the voice was flat, the eyes closed and the body bowed and rigid, as though he were kneeling before a priest instead of sitting before two sinners. Altogether he had a great look of Luke's portrait of Matthew, with the angel perched like a parrot on his shoulder.

" Almost madly in love with Miss Counihan some short weeks ago, now I do not even dislike her. Betrayed by Wylie in my trust and friendship, I do not even bother to forgive him. The missing Murphy from being a means to a trivial satisfaction, the contingent, as he himself would say, of a contingent, is become in himself an end, the end, my end, unique and indispensable."

The flow ceased. What truth has not its ballcock?

" The best of his knowledge," said Wylie.

" To the best of his ability," said Miss Counihan. " Fair is fair."

" Shall I shoot now or will you?" said Wylie.

" Do not wait for an answer," said Miss Counihan.

Wylie rose to his feet, hooked the thumb of his left hand in the armhole of his waistcoat, covered his præcordia with his right and said :

" This Neary that does not love Miss Counihan, nor need his Needle, any more, may he soon get over Murphy and find himself free, following his drift, to itch for an ape, or a woman writer."

" But this is Old Moore," said Miss Counihan, " not the *Weekly Irish Times.*"

" My attitude," said Wylie, " being the auscultation, execution and adequation of the voices, or rather voice, of Reason and Philautia, does not change. I continue to regard this Neary as a bull Io, born to be stung, Nature's gift to necessitous pimps ; Miss Counihan as the only nubile amateur to my certain knowledge in the Twenty-six Counties who does not confuse her self with her body, and one of the few bodies, in the same bog, equal to the distinction ; Murphy as a vermin at all costs to be avoided——"

Miss Counihan and Neary laughed profusely.

" He is so importunate," said Neary.

" So pushing," said Miss Counihan, " so thrusting."

" As an abomination," said Wylie, " the creepy thing that creepeth of the Law. Yet I pursue him."

" I pay you to," said Neary.

" Or so you hope," said Miss Counihan.

" Even so the beggar mutilates himself," said Wylie, " that he may live, and the beaver bites his off."

He sat down, stood up again immediately, resumed his pose and said :

" In a word I stand where I have always stood——"

" Since Heaven lay about you as a bedwetter," said Neary.

" And hope always to stand——"

" Until you drop," said Miss Counihan.

" Half on the make and half on pleasure bent."

He sat down again and Miss Counihan seized her opportunity, at just such intensity, pitch, quality and speed as could conveniently be worked up in the few words at her disposal.

" There is a mind and there is a body——"

" Shame ! " cried Neary. " Kick her arse ! Throw her out ! "

" On the one parched palm," said Wylie, " the swelling heart, the dwindling liver, the foaming spleen, two lungs with luck, with care two kidneys, and so on."

" And so forth," said Neary, with a sigh.

" And on the other," said Wylie, " the little ego and the big id."

" Infinite riches in a w.c.," said Neary.

" This ineffable counterpoint," continued Miss Counihan, " this mutual comment, this sole redeeming feature." She stopped in preference to being interrupted.

" She quite forgets how it goes on," said Wylie, " she will have to go right back to the beginning, like Darwin's caterpillar."

" Perhaps Murphy did not take her any further," said Neary.

" Everywhere I find defiled," continued Miss Counihan, " in the crass and unharmonious unison, the mind at the cart-tail of the body, the body at the chariot-wheels of the mind. I name no names."

" Excellent reception," said Wylie.

" No trace of fading," said Neary.

" Everywhere that is," concluded Miss Couni-han, " except where Murphy is. He did not suffer from this—er—psychosomatic fistula, Murphy my fiancé. Both mind and body, neither mind that is nor body, what can there be beside him, after him what could there be, but a puerile grossness or a senile agility? "

" Take your choice," said Wylie, " pick your fancy."

" Another semitone," said Neary, " and we had ceased to hear."

" Who knows but that we have? " said Wylie. " Who knows what dirty story, what even better dirty story, it may be even one we have not heard before, told at some colossal pitch of pure smut, beats at this moment in vain against our eardrums? "

" For me," said Neary, with the same sigh as before, " the air is always full of such, sough-ing with the bawdy innuendo of eternity."

Miss Counihan rose, gathered her things together, walked to the door and unlocked it with the key that she exiled for that purpose from her bosom. Standing in profile against the blazing corridor, with her high buttocks and her low breasts, she looked not merely queenly, but on for anything. And these impressions she enhanced by simply advancing one foot a pace, settling all her weight on the other, inclining her bust no more than was necessary to preserve her from falling down backwards and placing her hands upon her moons, plump and plain. In this position lightly but firmly poised she said, into her lap, in a voice like a distant rake on gravel in a winter gloaming :

" Now that we have let the cat out of the bag——"

" The pig out of the poke," said Wylie.

" How are we advantaged ? "

" Wylie," said Neary, " have a little consideration, you are right in her line of fire."

" The Goddess of Gout," said Wylie, " brooding over a Doan's Pill."

" Do not imagine for a moment I want you to go," said Neary, " but this little creature is manœuvring to see you home."

" Tut ! tut ! " said Wylie, " I may not be a trueborn jackeen, but I am better than nothing. My superiority to nothing has often been commented on."

" I repeat my question," said Miss Counihan, " and am prepared to do so again if necessary."

" If the cock does not crow then," said Wylie, " depend upon it the hen has not laid."

" But have I not said," said Neary, " now we can part? Surely that is a great advantage."

" Do you really mean to sit there and tell me," said Miss Counihan, " *me*, that you consider we are now met ? "

Wylie covered his ears, threw back his head and cried :

" Stop it ! Or is it too late ? "

High above his head he tossed his arms, set off in a rapid shuffle, seized Miss Counihan's hands, raised them gently clear of her rump. In a moment they would hit the trail.

" Who ever met," said Miss Counihan, not in the least perturbed apparently, " if it comes to that, that met not at first sight ? "

" There is only one meeting and parting," said Wylie. " The act of love."

" Fancy that ! " said Miss Counihan.

" Then each with and from himself," said Wylie, " as well as with and from the other."

" With and from him and herself," said Neary, " have a little conduction, Wylie. Remember a lady is present."

" You," said Wylie bitterly, " I was to find you not ungrateful. As no doubt also this poor girl."

" Not quite," said Miss Counihan. " I was merely not to find him ungrateful."

" Point three," said Neary in reply. " I do

not ask to speak to Murphy. Show him only to these eyes of flesh and the money is yours."

" He may feel," said Miss Counihan, " you can never tell, that having deceived him once, we are capable of doing so again."

" An obole on account," begged Wylie. " Charity edifieth."

" Point one," said Neary. " It does not require even as little as this celebrated act of love, if acts indeed can ever be of love, or love survive in acts, to bid one's neighbour the time of day, the smile and the nod on the way in at evening, the scowl and no nod on the way out at morning, in the way described by Wylie. And to meet and part in my sense exceeds the power of feeling, however tender, and of bodily motions, however expert."

He paused to be asked what his sense was. Wylie was the mug.

" The repudiation of the known," said Neary, " a purely intellectual operation of unspeakable difficulty."

" Perhaps you hadn't heard," said Wylie, " Hegel arrested his development."

" Point two," said Neary. " Far be it from me to sit here and suggest to Miss Counihan that we are now met. There are still things that even I do not say to a lady. But I think it is not a naiveté to hope that the ice has been broken, nor a presumption to count on the Almighty to pull off the rest."

The light in the corridor went out with a crash, Wylie reined in Miss Counihan against an abyss of blackness. Neary cast his voice into the dying ache of echoes :

" There He blows, or I am greatly mistaken."

Wylie felt suddenly tired of holding Miss Counihan's hands at precisely the same moment as she did of having them held, a merciful coincidence. He let them go and the dark swallowed her up. She leaned against the outer wall and sobbed distinctly. It had been a trying experience.

" Till to-morrow at ten," said Wylie. " Leave out your cheque-book."

" Do not leave me alone like this," said Neary, " crackling with sins, my lips still moist with impieties tossed off in the heat of controversy."

" You hear that storm of snivelling," said Wylie, " yet all you think of is yourself."

" Tell her from an old flicker," said Neary, " when you have licked them all away, that not one was idle."

After some further reproaches, to which he received no answer, Wylie went away with Miss Counihan.

A curious feeling had come over Neary, namely that he would not get through the night. He had felt this before, but never quite so strongly. In particular he felt that to move a muscle or utter a syllable would certainly prove fatal. He breathed with heavy caution through the long hours of darkness, trembled uncontrollably and clutched the chair-arms. He did not feel cold, far from it, nor unwell, nor in pain ; he simply had this alarming conviction that every second was going to announce itself the first of his last ten minutes or a quarter of an hour on earth. The number of seconds in one dark night is a simple calculation that the curious reader will work out for himself.

When Wylie called the following afternoon, four or five hours late, Neary's hair was white as snow, but he felt better in himself.

" A curious feeling came over me," he said, " just as you were leaving, that I was going to start dying."

" So you have," said Wylie. " You look like a Junior Fellow already."

" I think perhaps if I were to go out now," said Neary, " and mix a little with the canaille, it might do me good."

" Bloomsbury is on our way," said Wylie.
" Don't forget your cheque-book."

In Gower Street Wylie said :

" How do you feel now ? "

" *I* thank you," said Neary, " life does not
seem so precious."

Miss Counihan was handing it out to her
Hindu in a steady stream. He stood before
her in an attitude of considerable dejection,
his hands pressed tightly over his eyes. As
Neary and Wylie approached he made a wild
gesture of metaphysical liquidation and sprang
into a taxi that happened to be passing or, as
he firmly believed, was clocking off an inscrutable
schedule from all eternity.

" Poor fellow," said Miss Counihan. " He
is off to Millbank."

" And how are we this morning ? " said Neary
with horrible solicitude and a leer at Wylie.
" Lassata ? "

Wylie simpered.

They set off for Brewery Road in a taxi. For
fully one minute not a word was spoken. Then
Wylie said :

" After all, there is nothing like dead silence.
My one dread was lest our conversation of last
night should resume us where it left us off."

Miss Carridge flew to the window at the un-

wonted sound. No taxi had ever stopped in
good faith at her door, though one had done
so once by error, and another in derision. She
appeared on the threshold with a Bible in one
hand and a poker in the other.

"Have you a Mr. Murphy staying here?"
said Wylie.

"We have come all the way from Cork,"
said Neary, "we have torn ourselves away from
the groves of Blarney, for the sole purpose of
cajoling him in private."

"We are his very dear friends," said Miss
Counihan, "and our news his good, what is
more."

"Mr. Murphy," said Wylie, "the ruins of
the ruins of the broth of a boy."

"Mr. Murphy is away on business," said
Miss Carridge.

Wylie crammed his handkerchief into his
mouth.

"Do not watch him too narrowly," said Neary,
"and you will see him take it out of his ear."

"We expect him hourly," said Miss Carridge.

"What did I tell you?" said Miss Counihan.
"Sweating his soul out in the East End, so that
I may have all the little luxuries to which I am
accustomed."

Wylie took advantage of the confusion that

followed these words, Neary and Miss Carridge not knowing where to look and the eyes of Miss Counihan closed in an ecstasy of some kind, to take the silk handkerchief out of his ear, blow his nose, wipe his eyes and return it to his pocket. It might truly be said to have done the rounds, Wylie's silk handkerchief.

" But if you care to step in," said Miss Carridge, moving sportingly to one side, " *Mrs.* Murphy would see you I haven't a doubt, not a doubt."

Miss Counihan congratulated herself on having closed her eyes when she did. With closed eyes, she said to herself, one cannot go far wrong. Unless one is absolutely alone. Then it is not necessary to—er—blink at such a rate.

" If you are quite sure you are quite sure," said Wylie.

It was at this moment that they all caught simultaneously for the first time, and with common good breeding refrained from remarking, a waft of Miss Carridge's peculiarity. But now there was no turning back. They all felt that, as the door closed behind them.

So all things hobble together for the only possible.

Miss Carridge ushered them into the big room, where Murphy and Celia had met and parted so often, in a very house-proud manner.

For the char had never been in better form.
The lemon of the walls whined like Vermeer's ;
and even Miss Counihan, collapsed on one of
the Balzac chairs, was inclined to regret her
reflection in the linoleum. Similarly before
Claude's Narcissus in Trafalgar Square, high-
class whores with faces lately lifted have breathed
a malediction on the glass.

Without warning Neary exclaimed :

" At the best, nothing ; at the worst, this
again."

Miss Carridge looked shocked, as well she
might. Wester than the Isle of Man she had
never set foot.

" I hope," she said, " you like my little
apartment, to let, if I may say so."

" The considered verdict on the greater life,"
said Wylie, " of one who can imagine nothing
worse than the lesser. Hardly the artistic type,
you will say."

" We are the Engels sisters," said Miss Counihan, " come to stay."

Miss Carridge left her little apartment.

" Hark ! " said Wylie, pointing upward.

A soft swaggering to and fro was audible.

" Mrs. M.," said Wylie, " never still, made
restless by the protracted absence of her young,
her ambitious husband."

The footfalls came to an end.

"She pauses to lean out of the window," said Wylie. "Nothing will induce her to throw herself down till he actually heaves into view. She has a sense of style."

Neary's associations were normal to the point of tedium. He thought of salts of lemon on the steps of Wynn's Hotel, the livid colours of that old vision closed his eyes, a wild evening's green and yellow seen in a puddle.

"The Engels sisters," said Miss Carridge, "craving a word with you."

Celia, thank God for a Christian name at last, dragged her tattered bust back into the room, the old boy's.

"Bosom friends of Mr. Murphy," said Miss Carridge, "they came in a taxi."

Celia raised her face. This caused Miss Carridge to add, in some confusion :

"But I needn't tell you that. Forgive me."

"Ah yes, you need," said Celia, "omit no material circumstance, I implore you. I have been so busy, so busy, so absorbed, my swan crossword you know, Miss Carridge, seeking the rime, the panting syllable to rime with breath, that I have been dead to the voices of the street, dead and damned, Miss Carridge, the myriad voices."

Miss Carridge did not know which arm to feel more thankful for, the Bible or the poker. She tightened her hold evenly on each and said :

"Do not give way to despair, it is most wrong."

"When I think of what I was," said Celia, "who I was, what I am, and now dead, on a Sunday afternoon, with the sun singing, and the birds shining, to the voices of the STREET, then——"

"Be sober," said Miss Carridge, "hope to the end. Give yourself a bit of a wipe and come down."

Celia wrapped a waterproof of pale blush buff about her, but did not give herself the wipe.

"I have nothing to be ashamed of, or to lose."

Descending the stairs Miss Carridge pondered this saying. On the landing outside the big room, the landing where Celia had seen the old boy for the first time and last, she held up the poker and said :

"But everything to gain."

"Nothing to lose," said Celia. "Therefore nothing to gain."

A long look of fellow-feeling filled the space between them, with calm, pity and a touch of contempt. They leaned against it as against a solid wall of wool and looked at each other across it. Then they continued on their ways, Miss Carridge down what stairs remained, Celia into their old room.

Bereft of motion, their lees of finer feeling in a sudden swirl, Neary and Wylie sat and stared. Miss Counihan took one look and returned her gaze hastily to the linoleum. Wylie staggered reverently to his feet. Celia exposed herself formally with her back to the door, then walked right through them and sat down on the edge of the bed nearer the window, so that throughout the scene that follows Murphy's half of the bed is between her and them. Neary staggered reverently to his feet.

" I fear you are ill, Mrs. Murphy," said Miss Counihan.

" You wished to see me," said Celia.

Neary and Wylie, feeling more and more swine before a pearl, stood and stared. Miss Counihan advanced to the edge of the bed nearer the door, developing as she did so a small bundle of Murphy's letters into a fan. With this in her two hands she reached out across the bed, flirted it open and shut in a manner carefully calculated to annoy and said :

" Here at a glance you have our *bonam fidem* ;

and on closer inspection, whenever you please, my correspondent's deficiency in same."

Celia looked dully from the letters to Miss Counihan, and from Miss Counihan to her companions, and from those petrified figures to the letters again, and finally right away from so much dark flesh and word to the sky, under which she had nothing to lose. Then she lay down on the bed, not with any theatrical intention, but in pure obedience to a sudden strong desire to do so. The likelihood of its appearing theatrical, or even positively affected, would not have deterred her, if it had occurred to her. She stretched herself out at the ease of her body as naturally as though her solitude had been without spectators.

" One of the innumerable small retail re-deemers," sneered Miss Counihan, " lodging her pennyworth of pique in the post-golgothan kitty."

But for Murphy's horror of the mental belch, Celia would have recognised this phrase, if she had heard it.

Miss Counihan brought her letters together with the sound of a sharp faint explosion and marched back to her place. Neary fetched his chair resolutely to the head of the bed, in very fair imitation of a man whose mind is made up. And Wylie sat down with the air of a novice

at Divine Service, uncertain as to whether the
congregation ceasing in a soft perturbation to
stand is about to sit or kneel, and looking about
him wildly for a sign.

All four are now in position. They will not
move from where they now are until they find
a formula, a *status quo* agreeable to all.

" My dear Mrs. Murphy," said Neary in a
voice dripping with solicitude.

" If one of you would tell me simply what
you want," said Celia. " I cannot keep up
with fine words."

When Neary had finished it was dark in the
room. Simplicity is as slow as a hearse and as
long as a last breakfast.

" Errors and omissions excepted," said Miss
Counihan.

Wylie's eyes began to pain him.

" I am a prostitute," began Celia, speaking
from where she lay, and when she had finished
it was night in the room, that black night so
rich in acoustic properties, and on the landing,
to the infinite satisfaction of Miss Carridge.

" You poor thing," said Miss Counihan, " how
you must have suffered."

" Shall I put on the light ? " said Wylie, his
ravenous eyes in torment.

" If you do I shall close my eyes," said Miss

Counihan. "It is only in the dark that one can meet."

Few ditches were deeper than Miss Counihan, the widow woman's cruse was not more receptive. But Celia had not spoken and Wylie was raising his arm when the calm voice resumed its fall, no less slowly than before, but perhaps less surely. He withheld his hand, the little temporary gent and pure in heart.

"At first I thought I had lost him because I could not take him as he was. Now I do not flatter myself."

A rest.

"I was a piece out of him that he could not go on without, no matter what I did."

A rest.

"He had to leave me to be what he was before he met me, only worse, or better, no matter what I did."

A long rest.

"I was the last exile."

A rest.

"The last, if we are lucky."

So love is wont to end, in protasis, if it be love.

From where he sat Wylie switched on the light, the high dim yellow glim that Murphy, a strict non-reader, had installed, and glutted his eyes. While Miss Counihan on the contrary closed hers with an ostentation that flattened her face, to show that when she said a thing she meant it.

" I cannot believe he has left you," said Wylie.

" He will come back," said Neary.

" We shall be here to receive him," said Miss Counihan.

Her cot had a high rail all the way round. Mr. Willoughby Kelly came, smelling strongly of drink, knelt, grasped the bars and looked at her through them. Then she envied him, and he her. Sometimes he sang.

" Neary and I upstairs," said Wylie.

" I here with you," said Miss Counihan.

" Call the woman," said Neary.

Sometimes he sang :

> *Weep not, my wanton, smile upon my knee,*
> *When thou art old, there's grief enough for thee,*

etc. Other times :

> *Love is a prick, love is a sting,*
> *Love is a pretty pretty thing,*

etc. Other times, other songs. But most times he did not sing at all.

" She is at hand," said Wylie, " and has been for some little time, unless there is a real goat in the house as well."

It was Sunday, October the 20th, Murphy's night of duty had come. So all things limp together for the only possible.

11

LATE that afternoon, after many fruitless hours in the chair, it would be just about the time Celia was telling her story, M.M.M. stood suddenly for music, MUSIC, MUSIC, in brilliant, brevier and canon, or some such typographical scream, if the gentle compositor would be so friendly. Murphy interpreted this in his favour, for he had seldom been in such need of encouragement.

But in the night of Skinner's House, walking round and round at the foot of the cross among the shrouded instruments of recreation, having done one round and marking the prescribed pause of ten minutes before the next, he felt the gulf between him and them more strongly than at any time during his week of day duty. He felt it was very likely with them that craved to cross it as with them that dreaded to—they never did.

A round took ten minutes, all being well. If all was not well, if a patient had cut his throat, or required attention, then the extra time taken by the round was levied on the pause. For it was an inflexible rule of the M.M.M., laid down in terms so strong as to be almost abusive, that every patient, and not merely those on parchment (or on caution), should be visited at regular intervals of not more than twenty minutes throughout the night. If things were so bad that the round took ten minutes longer than it should, then there was no pause and all was in order. But if things were still worse and the round took eleven minutes longer than it should, and as less than no pause was unfortunately beyond the powers of even the smartest attendant, then the painful fact had simply to be faced once more, that man proposed, but God disposed, even in the Magdalen Mental Mercyseat.

The incidence of this higher law might have been reduced by the introduction at night of an emergency runner. But this would have run the Mercyseat into close on a pound a week, supposing the mug could have been found.

A clean round, facetiously called a " virgin ", was simplicity itself. The nurse had merely to depress a switch before each door, flooding the cell with light of such ferocity that the eyes of the sleeping and waking opened and closed respectively, satisfy himself with a glance through the judas that the patient looked good for another twenty minutes, switch off the light, press the indicator and pass.

The indicator was most ingenious. The indicator recorded the visit, together with the hours, minutes and seconds at which it was paid, on a switchboard in Bom's apartment. The indicator would have been still more ingenious if it had been activated by the light switch, or even by the judas shutter. For many and many were the visits recorded for Bom's inspection, and never paid, by nurses who were tired or indolent or sensitive or fed up or malicious or behind time or unwilling to shatter a patient's repose.

Bom was what is vulgarly called a sadist and encouraged what is vulgarly called sadism in his assistants. If during the day this energy could not be discharged with any great freedom even on those patients who submitted to it as part and parcel of the therapeutic voodoo, with still less freedom could it be discharged on those who regarded it as *hors d'œuvre*. These latter were reported to the R.M.S. as " uncooperative ', " not cooperating in the routine of the wards " or, in extreme cases, " resistive ". They were liable to get hell at night.

Murphy's first round had shown him what a mere phrase was Neary's " Sleep and Insomnia, the Phidias and Scopas of Fatigue ". It might

have held good in the dormitory of a young
ladies' academy, where quite possibly also it had
been inspired, but it had no sense in the wards
of the M.M.M. Here those that slept and those
that did not were quite palpably by the same
hand, that of some rather later artist whose work
could by no means have come down to us, say
the Pergamene Barlach. And in his efforts to
distinguish between the two groups Murphy was
reminded of a wild waning winter afternoon in
Toulon before the *hôtel de ville* and Puget's
caryatids of Strength and Weariness, and the
tattered sky blackening above his perplexity as
to which was which.

Those that slept did so in the frozen attitudes
of Herculaneum, as though sleep had pounced
upon them like an act of God. And those that
did not did not by the obvious grace of the same
authority. The contortions of the resistive in
particular seemed to Murphy not so much an
entreaty to nature's soft nurse as a recoil from
her solicitations. The economy of care was
better served, in the experience of the resistive,
when they knit up the sleave by day.

By day he had not felt the gulf so painfully
as he did now, walking round and round the
wreck. By day there was Bom and other staff,
there were the doctors and the visitors, to

stimulate his sense of kindred with the patients. There were the patients themselves, circulating through the wards and in the gardens. He could mix with them, touch them, speak to them, watch them, imagine himself one of them. But in the night of Skinner's there were none of these admin- icles, no loathing to love from, no kick from the world that was not his, no illusion of caress from the world that might be. It was as though the microcosmopolitans had locked him out. No sound reached him from the adjacent female wards but the infinite variety of those made by the female wardees, a faint blurred mockery, from which however as the night wore on a number of leading motifs emerged. Ditto for the male wards below. The cackle of a nightin- gale would have been most welcome, to explode his spirit towards its nightingaleless night. But the season seemed over.

In short there was nothing but he, the unin- telligible gulf and they. That was all. All. ALL.

It was therefore with a heavy heart that he set out on round two. The first cell to be revisited, that at the south-westernmost corner of the nave, contained Mr. Endon, voted by one and all the most biddable little gaga in the entire institution, his preoccupation with apnœa notwithstanding.

Murphy switched on the thousand candles, shot back the judas shutter and looked in. A strange sight met his eye.

Mr. Endon, an impeccable and brilliant figurine in his scarlet gown, his crest a gush of vivid white against the black shag, squatted tailor-fashion on the head of his bed, holding his left foot in his right hand and in his left hand his right foot. The purple poulaines were on his feet and the rings were on his fingers. The light spurted off Mr. Endon north, south, east, west and in fifty-six other directions. The sheet stretched away before him, as smooth and taut as a groaning wife's belly, and on it a game of chess was set up. The little blue and olive face, wearing an expression of winsome fiat, was upturned to the judas.

Murphy resumed his round, gratified in no small measure. Mr. Endon had recognised the feel of his friend's eye upon him and made his preparations accordingly. Friend's eye? Say rather, Murphy's eye. Mr. Endon had felt Murphy's eye upon him. Mr. Endon would have been less than Mr. Endon if he had known what it was to have a friend ; and Murphy more than Murphy if he had not hoped against his better judgment that his feeling for Mr. Endon was in some small degree reciprocated. Whereas

the sad truth was, that while Mr. Endon for
Murphy was no less than bliss, Murphy for Mr.
Endon was no more than chess.   Murphy's eye ?
Say rather, the chessy eye. Mr. Endon had
vibrated to the chessy eye upon him and made
his preparations accordingly.

Murphy completed his round, an Irish virgin.
(Finished on time a round was called a virgin ;
ahead of time, an Irish virgin.)   The hypomanic
it is true, in pad since morning with a big attack
blowing up, had tried to come at his tormentor
through the judas. This distressed Murphy,
though he rather disliked the hypomanic. But
it did not delay him. Quite the reverse.

He hastened back westward down the nave
with his master key at the ready. He stopped
short of the wreck, switched on Mr. Endon's
light and entered bodily into his cell. Mr.
Endon was in the same position all but his head,
which was now bowed, whether over the board
or merely on his chest it was hard to say. Murphy
sank down on his elbow on the foot of the bed
and the game began.

Murphy's functions were scarcely affected by
this break with the tradition of night duty. All
it meant was that he took his pauses with Mr.
Endon instead of in the wreck. Every ten
minutes he left the cell, pressed the indicator

with heartfelt conviction and did a round. Every ten minutes and sometimes even sooner, for never in the history of the M.M.M. had there been such a run of virgins and Irish virgins as on this Murphy's maiden night, he returned to the cell and resumed the game. Sometimes an entire pause would pass without any change having been made in the position ; and at other times the board would be in an uproar, a torrent of moves.

The game, an Endon's Affence, or *Zwei-springerspott*, was as follows :

White (MURPHY)	Black (MR. ENDON) (a)
1. P—K4 (b)	1. Kt—KR3
2. Kt—KR3	2. R—KKt1
3. R—KKt1	3. Kt—QB3
4. Kt—QB3	4. Kt—K4
5. Kt—Q5 (c)	5. R—KR1
6. R—KR1	6. Kt—QB3
7. Kt—QB3	7. Kt—KKt1
8. Kt—QKt1	8. Kt—QKt1 (d)
9. Kt—KKt1	9. P—K3
10. P—KKt3 (e)	10. Kt—K2
11. Kt—K2	11. Kt—KKt3
12. P—KKt4	12. B—K2
13. Kt—KKt3	13. P—Q3
14. B—K2	14. Q—Q2
15. P—Q3	15. K—Q1 (f)
16. Q—Q2	16. Q—K1
17. K—Q1	17. Kt—Q2
18. Kt—QB3 (g)	18. R—QKt1
19. R—QKt1	19. Kt—QKt3
20. Kt—QR4	20. B—Q2

21.	P—QKt3	21.	R—KKt1
22.	R—KKt1	22.	K—QB1 (h)
23.	B—QKt2	23.	Q—KB1
24.	K—QB1	24.	B—K1
25.	B—QB3 (i)	25.	Kt—KR1
26.	P—QKt4	26.	B—Q1
27.	Q—KR6 (j)	27.	Kt—QR1 (k)
28.	Q—KB6	28.	Kt—KKt3
29.	B—K5	29.	B—K2
30.	Kt—QB5 (l)	30.	K—Q1 (m)
31.	Kt—KR1 (n)	31.	B—Q2
32.	K—QKt2 ! !	32.	R—KR1
33.	K—QKt3	33.	B—QB1
34.	K—QR4	34.	Q—K1 (o)
35.	K—R5	35.	Kt—QKt3
36.	B—KB4	36.	Kt—Q2
37.	Q—QB3	37.	R—QR1
38.	Kt—QR6 (p)	38.	B—KB1
39.	K—QKt5	39.	Kt—K2
40.	K—QR5	40.	Kt—QKt1
41.	Q—QB6	41.	Kt—KKt1
42.	K—QKt5	42.	K—K2 (q)
43.	K—R5	43.	Q—Q1 (r)

And White surrenders.

(a) Mr. Endon always played Black. If presented with White he would fade, without the least trace of annoyance, away into a light stupor.

(b) The primary cause of all White's subsequent difficulties.

(c) Apparently nothing better, bad as this is.

(d) An ingenious and beautiful début, sometimes called the Pipe-opener.

(e) Ill-judged.

(f) Never seen in the Café de la Régence, seldom in Simpson's Divan.

(g) The flag of distress.

(h) Exquisitely played.

(*i*) It is difficult to imagine a more deplorable situation than poor White's at this point.

(*j*) The ingenuity of despair.

(*k*) Black has now an irresistible game.

(*l*) High praise is due to White for the pertinacity with which he struggles to lose a piece.

(*m*) At this point Mr. Endon, without as much as "j'adoube", turned his King and Queen's Rook upside down, in which position they remained for the rest of the game.

(*n*) A *coup de repos* long overdue.

(*o*) Mr. Endon not crying " Check ! ", nor otherwise giving the slightest indication that he was alive to having attacked the King of his opponent, or rather vis-à-vis, Murphy was absolved, in accordance with Law 18, from attending to it. But this would have been to admit that the salute was adventitious.

(*p*) No words can express the torment of mind that goaded White to this abject offensive.

(*q*) The termination of this solitaire is very beautifully played by Mr. Endon.

(*r*) Further solicitation would be frivolous and vexatious, and Murphy, with fool's mate in his soul, retires.

Following Mr. Endon's forty-third move Murphy gazed for a long time at the board before laying his Shah on his side, and again for a long time after that act of submission. But little by little his eyes were captured by the brilliant swallow-tail of Mr. Endon's arms and legs, purple, scarlet, black and glitter, till they saw nothing else, and that in a short time only as a vivid blur, Neary's big blooming buzzing confusion or ground, mercifully free of figure.

Wearying soon of this he dropped his head on his arms in the midst of the chessmen, which scattered with a terrible noise. Mr. Endon's finery persisted for a little in an after-image scarcely inferior to the original. Then this also faded and Murphy began to see nothing, that colourlessness which is such a rare postnatal treat, being the absence (to abuse a nice distinction) not of *percipere* but of *percipi*. His other senses also found themselves at peace, an unexpected pleasure. Not the numb peace of their own suspension, but the positive peace that comes when the somethings give way, or perhaps simply add up, to the Nothing, than which in the guffaw of the Abderite naught is more real. Time did not cease, that would be asking too much, but the wheel of rounds and pauses did, as Murphy with his head among the armies continued to suck in, through all the posterns of his withered soul, the accidentless One-and-Only, conveniently called Nothing. Then this also vanished, or perhaps simply came asunder, in the familiar variety of stenches, asperities, ear-splitters and eye-closers, and Murphy saw that Mr. Endon was missing.

For quite some little time Mr. Endon had been drifting about the corridors, pressing here a light-switch and there an indicator, in a way that seemed haphazard but was in fact determined

by an amental pattern as precise as any of those
that governed his chess. Murphy found him in
the south transept, gracefully stationed before
the hypomanic's pad, ringing the changes on the
various ways in which the indicator could be
pressed and the light turned on and off. Beginning with the light turned off to begin with he
had : lit, indicated, extinguished ; lit, extinguished, indicated ; indicated, lit, extinguished.
Continuing then with the light turned on to
begin with he had : extinguished, lit, indicated ;
extinguished, indicated, lit ; indicated, extinguished and was seriously thinking of lighting
when Murphy stayed his hand.

The hypomanic bounced off the walls like a
bluebottle in a jar.

Bom's switchboard the following morning
informed him that the hypomanic had been
visited at regular intervals of ten minutes from
8 p.m. till shortly after 4 a.m., then for nearly
an hour not at all, then six times in the space
of one minute, then no more. This unprecedented distribution of visits had a lasting effect
on Bom and continued to baffle his ingenuity up
to and including the day of his death. He gave
it out that Murphy had gone mad, and even
went so far as to say that he was not surprised.
This went some way towards saving the credit

of his department, but none at all towards setting his own mind at rest. And the Magdalen Mental Mercyseat remembers Murphy to this day, with pity, derision, contempt and a touch of awe, as the male nurse that went mad with his colours nailed to the mast. This affords him no consolation. He is in no need of any.

Mr. Endon went quietly, back to his cell. It was of no consequence to Mr. Endon that his hand had been stayed from restoring his Shah to his square, and the hypomanic's light from off to on. It was a fragment of Mr. Endon's good fortune not to be at the mercy of the hand, whether another's or his own.

Murphy put the men back into the box, took off Mr. Endon's gown and slippers and tucked him up in bed. Mr. Endon lay back and fixed his eyes on some object immeasurably remote, perhaps the famous ant on the sky of an airless world. Murphy kneeled beside the bed, which was a low one, took Mr. Endon's head in his hands and brought the eyes to bear on his, or rather his on them, across a narrow gulf of air, the merest hand's-breadth of air. Murphy had often inspected Mr. Endon's eyes, but never with such close and prolonged attention as now.

In shape they were remarkable, being both deep-set and protuberant, one of Nature's jokes involving sockets so widely splayed that Mr. Endon's brows and cheekbones seemed to have subsided. And in colour scarcely less so, having almost none. For the whites, of which a sliver appeared below the upper lid, were very large indeed and the pupils prodigiously dilated, as though by permanent excess of light. The iris was reduced to a thin glaucous rim of spawnlike consistency, so like a ballrace between the black and white that these could have started to rotate in opposite directions, or better still the same direction, without causing Murphy the least surprise. All four lids were everted in an ectropion of great expressiveness, a mixture of cunning, depravity and rapt attention. Approaching his eyes still nearer Murphy could see the red frills of mucus, a large point of suppuration at the root of an upper lash, the filigree of veins like the Lord's Prayer on a toenail and in the cornea, horribly reduced, obscured and distorted, his own image. They were all set, Murphy and Mr. Endon, for a butterfly kiss, if that is still the correct expression.

Kneeling at the bedside, the hair starting in thick black ridges between his fingers, his lips, nose and forehead almost touching Mr. Endon's, seeing himself stigmatised in those eyes that did not see him, Murphy heard words demanding so strongly to be spoken that he spoke them, right into Mr. Endon's face, Murphy who did not speak at all in the ordinary way unless spoken to, and not always even then.

> " the last at last seen of him
> himself unseen by him
> and of himself "

A rest.

" The last Mr. Murphy saw of Mr. Endon was Mr. Murphy unseen by Mr. Endon. This was also the last Murphy saw of Murphy."

A rest.

" The relation between Mr. Murphy and Mr. Endon could not have been better summed up than by the former's sorrow at seeing himself in the latter's immunity from seeing anything but himself."

A long rest.

" Mr. Murphy is a speck in Mr. Endon's unseen."

That was the whole extent of the little afflatulence. He replaced Mr. Endon's head firmly on the pillow, rose from his knees, left the cell, and the building, without reluctance and without relief.

In contrast with the foredawn which was pitch black, cold and damp, Murphy felt incandescent. An hour previously the moon had been obliged to set, and the sun could not rise for an hour to come. He raised his face to the starless sky, abandoned, patient, the sky, not the face, which was abandoned only. He took off his shoes and socks and threw them away. He set off slowly, trailing his feet, through the long grass among the trees towards the male nurses' quarters. He took off his clothes one by one as he went, quite forgetting they did not belong to him, and threw them away. When he was naked he lay down in a tuft of soaking tuffets and tried to get a picture of Celia. In vain. Of his mother. In vain. Of his father (for he was not illegitimate). In vain. It was usual for him to fail with his mother ; and usual, though less usual, for him to fail with a woman. But never before had he failed with his father. He saw the clenched fists and rigid upturned face of the Child in a Giovanni Bellini Circumcision, waiting to feel the knife. He saw eyeballs being scraped, first any eyeballs, then Mr. Endon's. He tried again with his father, his mother, Celia, Wylie, Neary, Cooper, Miss Dew, Miss Carridge, Nelly, the sheep, the chandlers, even Bom and Co., even Bim, even Ticklepenny and Miss Counihan, even Mr. Quigley. He tried with the men, women, children and animals that belong to even worse stories than this. In vain in all cases. He could not

get a picture in his mind of any creature he had
met, animal or human. Scraps of bodies, of
landscapes, hands, eyes, lines and colours evoking
nothing, rose and climbed out of sight before
him, as though reeled upward off a spool level
with his throat. It was his experience that this
should be stopped, whenever possible, before the
deeper coils were reached. He rose and hastened
to the garret, running till he was out of breath,
then walking, then running again, and so on.
He drew up the ladder, lit the dip sconced in its
own grease on the floor and tied himself up in
the chair, dimly intending to have a short rock
and then, if he felt any better, to dress and go,
before the day staff were about, leaving Ticklepenny to face the music, MUSIC, MUSIC, back to
Brewery Road, to Celia, serenade, nocturne,
albada. Dimly, very dimly. He pushed off. A
phrase from Suk joined in the rhythm. "The
square of Moon and Solar Orb afflicts the Hyleg.
Herschel in Aquarius stops the water." At one
of the rock's dead points he saw, for a second,
far beneath, the dip and radiator, gleam and
grin ; at the other the skylight, open to no stars.
Slowly he felt better, astir in his mind, in the
freedom of that light and dark that did not clash,
nor alternate, nor fade nor lighten except to
their communion. The rock got faster and faster,

shorter and shorter, the gleam was gone, the grin was gone, the starlessness was gone, soon his body would be quiet. Most things under the moon got slower and slower and then stopped, a rock got faster and faster and then stopped. Soon his body would be quiet, soon he would be free.

The gas went on in the w.c., excellent gas, superfine chaos.

Soon his body was quiet.

12

Forenoon, Wednesday, October the 23rd. Not
a cloud left in the sky.

Cooper sat—*sat!*—beside the driver, Wylie
between Celia and Miss Counihan, Neary on
one bracket-seat with his legs on the other and
his back against the door, a very perilous position for Neary. Neary considered himself better
off than Wylie because he could see Celia's face,
which was turned to the window. And Wylie
considered himself better off than Neary, especially when they came to a cobbled surface
or turned a corner. Faces held up Neary a
little longer than they did Wylie.

Miss Counihan's face was also turned to the
window, but in vain, as she read there unmistakably. This did not greatly trouble her.
They would never get any more than they
were getting now, which she did not do them
the credit of assessing at a very large amount.
Indeed, they would never again get as much
as the little that would shortly be with-

drawn. Then they would come ramping to her again.

Miss Counihan could think ill of her partners, past, present and prospective, without prejudice to herself. This is a faculty that no young man or woman, stepping down into the sexpit, should be without.

For all except Celia, whose affective mechanisms seemed to be arrested, it was like being in the chief mourners' cab, so strong was the feeling of getaway. Indeed, Brewery Road had become intolerable. The old endless chain of love, tolerance, indifference, aversion and disgust.

Miss Counihan would not have minded going up to Wylie if Celia had not minded Neary coming down to her. Nor would Wylie have objected in the least to going down to Celia if Miss Counihan had not objected most strongly to going up to Neary. Nor would Neary have been less than delighted to go down to either, or have either come up to him, if both had not been more than averse to his attentions, whether on the first floor or the second.

Accordingly Celia and Miss Counihan continued to share the bed in the big room, the latter shedding lights on Murphy that were no credit to herself and no news to the former ; and Neary and Wylie to take spells in the bed in the old boy's room, each evoking Celia according to his disposition.

So Neary and Celia cease slowly to need Murphy. He, that he may need her; she, that she may rest from need.

To cap all Cooper was given a shakedown in the kitchen. Through the keyhole Miss Carridge watched him, settling down for the night in his socks, moleskins, shirt and hat. A dull coucher for Miss Carridge.

For two days and three nights they did not leave the house. Neary, because distrusting his associates singly and as a pair he feared lest Murphy should arrive while he was absent; Wylie and Miss Counihan, for the same reason; Cooper, because he was forbidden; Celia, because it did not occur to her; Miss Carridge, because she had no time. It seemed as though none of them would ever go out again, when relief arrived in the shape of an assurance from Dr. Angus Killiecrankie that so far as the fear of missing Murphy was concerned, they might all take the air without the least anxiety.

Nothing was said on the way down. For the little they knew of the little they felt could with no more propriety be acknowledged than denied. Celia leaning back with her face to the window was aware only of all the colours

of light streaming back into the past and the
seat thrusting her forward. Miss Counihan
pressed her bosom with vague relish against
the lesser of two evils that had befallen her. So
long as she had not lost Murphy thus beyond
recall, the risk subsisted of his setting her simply
aside without more, which would have been
bad, or in favour of Celia, which would have
been awful, or of some other slut, which would
have been pretty bad also. In a somewhat
similar way Neary, for whom the sight of Celia
had restored Murphy from being an end in
himself to his initial condition of obstacle (or
key), had cause to be pleased with the turn
events had taken. And to Wylie, between jolts
and corners, the only phrase to propose itself
was : " Didn't I tell you she would lead us
to him ? " But politeness and candour run
together, when one is not fitting neither is the
other. Then the occasion calls for silence, that
frail partition between the ill-concealed and the
ill-revealed, the clumsily false and the unavoidably so.

They were received at the Mercyseat by Dr.
Angus Killiecrankie, the Outer Hebridean
R.M.S., an eminescent home county authority
and devout Mottist. He was a large, bony,
stooping, ruddy man, bluff but morose, with

an antiquary's cowl whiskers, mottled market-gardener's hands thickly overlaid with pink lanugo, and eyes red with straining for degenerative changes. He tucked up his whiskers and said :

" Mrs. Murrphy ? "

" I fear we were just his very dear friends," said Miss Counihan.

Dr. Killiecrankie drew a singed envelope from his pocket and held it up with the air of a conjuror displaying the ace. It bore the name Mrs. Murphy and the address in Brewery Road, pencilled in laborious capitals.

" This was all we had to go on," he said. " If he had any other papers, they were consoomed."

Neary, Wylie and Miss Counihan flung out their hands with one accord.

" I'll see she gets it," said Neary.

" Without fail," said Wylie.

" His very dear friends," said Miss Counihan.

Dr. Killiecrankie put up the envelope and led the way.

The mortuary was at its bungaloidest, the traveller's joy gleamed wanly with its pale old wood, the scarlet ampelopsis quenched the brick. Bim and Ticklepenny were sitting cheek by jowl on the dazzling granite step, and out in the middle of the forecourt of lawn a short but willowy male figure, dressed wearily in black and striped, his lithe bowler laid crown downwards on the grass beside him, was making violent golfing movements with his umbrella. Appearances were not deceptive, it was the county coroner.

They entered the mortuary, when the little duel between R.M.S and coroner as to which would pass second had been amicably settled without dishonour, in the following order : R.M.S. and coroner, twined together ; Neary ; Miss Counihan ; Celia ; Wylie ; Cooper ; Ticklepenny and Bim, wreathed together. They proceeded directly along a short passage, flanked on either hand with immense double-decker refrigerators, six in all, to the post-mortem room, a sudden lancination of white and silver, to the north an unbroken bay of glass frosted to a height of five feet from the floor and reaching to the ceiling. Outside the horns of yew had the hopeless harbour-mouth look, the arms of two that can reach no further, or of one in supplication, the patient impotence of charity or prayer.

Bim and Ticklepenny paused in the passage to collect Murphy. They slid him out on his aluminium tray, they carried him into the p.m.

room, they laid him out on the slab of ruin
marble in the key of the bay. In the narrow
space to the north of the slab Dr. Killiecrankie
and the coroner took up the demonstrative
attitude. Bim and Ticklepenny awaited the
signal at the head and foot of the tray, the
four corners of the sheet gathered in their hands.
The rest drooped in a crescent near the door.
Celia watched a brown stain on the shroud
where the iron had scorched it. Wylie supported Miss Counihan, mistress of the graded
swoon, who closed her eyes and murmured,
"Tell me when to look." Neary remarking
with a shock that Cooper had taken off his hat
and that his head was apparently quite normal,
except that the hair was perhaps rather more
abundant than is usual in men of Cooper's age,
and horribly matted, suddenly realised that
Cooper had sat all the way from Brewery
Road.

"These remains," said the coroner in his
nancy soprano, "were deposited just within
my county, my county, I am most heartily
sorry to say. Another long putt and I would
be sinking them now."

He closed his eyes and struck a long putt.
The ball left the club with the sweet sound of
a flute, flowed across the green, struck the back

of the tin, spouted a foot into the air, fell plumb into the hole, bubbled and was still. He sighed and hurried on :

" My function perhaps it is part of my duty to inform you is to determine, one, who is dead, and, two, how. With regard to the latter matter, the latter matter, happily it need not detain us, thanks to the, how shall I say——? "

" The irrrefragable post-mortem appearance," said Dr. Killiecrankie. " Mr. Clinch, please."

Bim and Ticklepenny lifted the sheet. Celia started forward.

" One moment," said Dr. Killiecrankie. " Thank you, Mr. Clinch."

Bim and Ticklepenny lowered the sheet. Celia remained standing a little in advance of the others.

" I say shock following burns," said the coroner, " without the slightest hesitation."

" Not the slightest," said Dr. Killiecrankie.

" Death by burns," said the coroner, " perhaps I am expected to add, is a wholly unscientific condition. Burns always shocks, I beg your pardon, my dear Angus, always shock, some-times more, sometimes less, according to their strength, their locus and the shockability of the burner. The same is true of scalds."

" Sepsis does not arise," said Dr. Killiecrankie.

" My physiology is rather rusty," said the coroner, " but no doubt it was not required."

" We arrived too late for sepsis to arise," said Dr. Killiecrankie. " The shock was ample."

" Then suppose we say severe shock following burns," said the coroner, " to be absolutely clear."

" Yes," said Dr. Killiecrankie, " or severe shock following severe burrrns. I do not think that is too strong."

" By all means," said the coroner, " severe burns let it be, followed by severe shock. So much for the *modus morendi*, the *modus morendi*."

" An accident ? " said Neary.

The coroner stood quite still for a moment with the stupefied, almost idiot, expression of one who is not quite sure if a joke has been made, nor, if so, in what it consists. Then he said :

" I beg your pardon."

Neary repeated his question, on a rising note. The coroner opened and closed his mouth a number of times, threw up his arms and turned aside. But words never failed Dr. Killiecrankie, that for him would have been tantamount to loose thinking, so up went the whiskers.

" A classical case of misadventure."

Unromantic to the last, thought Miss Counihan. She had taken out her leaving certificate.

" Before we get completely out of our depth,"
said the coroner, " perhaps there is something
else the gentleman here would like to know.
Whether for example it was a Brymay safety
that exploded the mixture, or a wax vesta.
Such poor lights as I possess are his to extinguish."

Neary attended to his nose with studied in-
solence. Wylie felt proud of his acquaintance,
for the first time.

" Then perhaps I may venture to proceed,"
said the coroner, " to the other matter, the
identity of the ac—the deceased. Here I need
hardly say we find ourselves embarrassed by
that very feature of the—the——"

" Tragic occurrence," said Dr. Killiecrankie.

" Very feature of the tragic occurrence that
stood us in such good stead in the matter of
the manner of death. The matter of the manner
of death. Still we must not complain. What
does the poet say, Angus, perhaps you remember ? "

" What poet ? " said Dr. Killiecrankie.

" ' Never the rose without the thorn '," said
the coroner. " I quote from memory, bitter
memory."

" Mr. Clinch, please," said Dr. Killiecrankie.

Bim and Ticklepenny reached forward with
their corners, Bim received the shroud in folio,

converted it deftly into octavo, and both stood back. The very dear friends moved up to the slab, Celia in the centre and still a little to the fore.

" By all accounts," said the coroner, " if I may say so without prejudice, it was a person abounding in distinctive marks, both mental and physical. But——"

" You forget the moral," sneered Dr. Killie-crankie, " and the spiritual, or as some say, functional."

" But whether——"

" Remarkable for the pertinacity," said Dr. Killiecrankie, " with which they elude the closest autopsy."

" But whether any of these have survived the conflagration," continued the coroner, " is a question that I for one, and I should imagine all those who were not of the inner circle, cannot presume to decide. It is here that you may help us."

Such a silence followed these words that the faint hum of the refrigerators could be heard. The eyes of all, seventeen in all, strayed and mingled among the remains.

How various are the ways of looking away ! Bim and Ticklepenny raised their heads to-gether, their eyes met in a look both tender and ardent, they were alive and well and had each other. Dr. Killiecrankie slowly sunk his head, till he was nothing but legs, skull and whiskers. He owed not a little of his reputation to this gift of seeming to brood when in fact his mind was entirely blank. The coroner did not move his head, he simply let go the focus and ceased to see. Neary and Wylie diverted their attention calmly to other things, the appointments of the room, beyond the glass the bright green and the dark green, leaning on the blue of heaven. The disclaimer was evident. One rapid glance from his solitary eye was enough for Cooper, whom the least little thing upset. Miss Counihan looked away and back, away and back, surprised and pleased to find she was of such stern stuff, annoyed that no trace remained of what she had known, chagrined that she could not exclaim, before them all, pointing to her justification : " This is Murphy, whose very dear friend I was." Celia alone seemed capable of giving her undivided attention to the matter in hand, her eyes continued to move patiently, gravely and intently among the remains long after the others had ceased to look, long after Miss Counihan herself had despaired of establishing the closeness of her acquaintance.

From his dream of pins split and bunkers

set at nought the coroner came to with a start
and said :

" Any luck ? "

" Could you turn him over ? " said Celia, her
first words for fully sixty hours, her first request
for longer than she could have remembered.

" By all means," said the coroner, " though
I fancy you have seen the best of him."

" Mr. Clinch," said Dr. Killiecrankie.

The remains having been turned over, Celia
addressed herself with a suddenly confident
air to the further of the charred buttocks and
found at once what she sought. She put her
finger lightly on the spot and said :

" Here he had a big birthmark."

Coroner and R.M.S. pounced on the find.

" Beyond the slightest doubt," said Dr. Killiecrankie, " an extensive capillary angioma of
most unusual situation."

" A proper port-winer," said the coroner.
" The afterglow is unmistakable."

Miss Counihan burst into tears.

" I knew of no such mark," she cried, " I
don't believe he ever had a horrid mark like
that, I don't believe it's my Murphy at all, it
doesn't look at *all* like him, I don't believe——"

" There there," said Neary. " There there.
There there."

" How beautiful in a way," said the coroner,
" birthmark deathmark, I mean, rounding off
the life somehow, don't you think, full circle,
you know, eh, Angus ? "

" There there," said Neary. " No man is
without blemish."

" Well," said the coroner, " now that we
know who is dead, who is ? "

" Mr. Murphy," said Neary, " native of the
city of Dublin."

" Dear old indelible Dublin," said the coroner.
" Our only female link passed peacefully away
in the Coombe, a month and a half before her
time, under the second George. Christian name.
Next-of-kin."

" None," said Neary. " A Dutch uncle."

" Who the devil are you ? " said the coroner.

" His very dear friends," said Miss Counihan.
" His dearest friends."

" How often have you to be told ? " said Wylie.

" Was it to Murphy he answered," said the
coroner, " or only to Mr. Murphy ? "

" Mr. Clinch," said Dr. Killiecrankie.

They covered the tray and carried it out
to the refrigerators. Neary saw Clonmachnois
on the slab, the castle of the O'Melaghlins,
meadow, eskers, thatch on white, something
red, the wide bright water, Connaught.

"And this young lady," said the coroner, "who knew him in such detail, such opportune detail——"

"Miss Celia Kelly," said Neary.

"Did Miss Kelly murmur Murphy," said the coroner, "or Mr. Murphy?"

"Damn you and blast you," said Neary, "the man was unbaptised. What the bloody hell more do you want?"

"And this Mrs. Murrrphy," said Dr. Killiecrankie, "who was she? The Dutch uncle?"

"There is no Mrs. Murphy," said Neary.

"An epigram," said the coroner, "has been attempted."

"Miss Kelly would have been Mrs. Murphy," said Neary, "if Mr. Murphy had been spared a little longer."

"One would have thought so," said the coroner.

Cooper and Wylie supported Miss Counihan.

"No," said Celia.

With a bow Dr. Killiecrankie handed the letter to Celia, who handed it to Neary, who opened it, read, reread, hesitated, read again and said at last:

"With Miss Kelly's permission . . ."

"Is there anything more?" said Celia. "I should like to go."

" This may concern you," said Dr. Killiecrankie, " since it appears to be addressed to
you."

Neary read out :

" With regard to the disposal of these my body,
mind and soul, I desire that they be burnt and
placed in a paper bag and brought to the Abbey
Theatre, Lr. Abbey Street, Dublin, and without pause
into what the great and good Lord Chesterfield calls
the necessary house, where their happiest hours have
been spent, on the right as one goes down into the
pit, and I desire that the chain be there pulled upon
them, if possible during the performance of a piece,
the whole to be executed without ceremony or show
of grief."

Neary continued to gaze on the sheet for
some time after he had ceased to read. At
last he put it back in the envelope and handed
it to Celia, who grasped it to tear it across,
remembered her solitude was not without
witnesses and contented herself for the time
being with crumpling it in the palm of her
hand.

" The necessary house," said the coroner,
catching up his hat and umbrella.

" Their happiest hours," groaned Miss Counihan. " When is it dated ? "

" Burnt," said Wylie.

" Body and all," said Dr. Killiecrankie.

Bim and Ticklepenny had gone, already they were far away, behind a tree, in the sun.

" Leave me among the slops," begged Ticklepenny, " do not send me back to the wards."

" Darling," said Bim, " that is entirely up to you."

The coroner had gone, he unbuttoned his black and striped with one hand and drove with the other, sweater and slacks would soon enfold him.

Celia was going.

" Just one moment," said Dr. Killiecrankie. " What arrangements do you wish to make ? "

" Arrangements ? " said Neary.

" The essence of all cold storage," said Dr. Killiecrankie, " is a free turrnover. I need every refrigerator."

" I shall be outside," said Celia.

Neary and Wylie listened for the sound of the outer door opened and closed. It did not come and Neary stopped listening. Then it came, neither loudly nor softly, and Wylie stopped listening.

" Surely his last wish is sacred," said Miss Counihan. " Surely we are bound to honour it."

" Hardly his last, I fancy," said Wylie, " all things considered."

" Do you incinerate here ? " said Neary.

Dr. Killiecrankie confessed to a small close furnace of the reverberatory type, in which the toughest body, mind and soul could be relied on to revert, in under an hour, for the negligible sum of thirty shillings, to ash of an eminently portable quantity.

Neary slapped down his cheque-book on the slab, wrote four cheques and handed them round. To Miss Counihan and Wylie he said good-bye, to Cooper " Wait ", to Dr. Killiecrankie, " I trust you will accept my cheque."

" Accompanied by your card," said Dr. Killiecrankie. " Thank you."

" When it is ready," said Neary, " give it to this man, and to no one else."

" This is all rather irregular," said Dr. Killiecrankie.

" Life is all rather irregular," said Neary.

Miss Counihan and Wylie had gone. The scarlet leaves drooped over them, they consulted together. Neary had not distinguished between their services, or their sexes, but had been not ungenerous with an even hand. She, in obedience to an impulse of long standing, seized him passionately by the Fifty Shilling lapels and cried :

" Do not leave me, oh do not walk out on me at this unspeakable juncture."

She impeded his view, he caught her by the wrists, she tightened her hold and continued.

" Oh hand in hand let us return to the dear land of our birth, the bays, the bogs, the moors, the glens, the lakes, the rivers, the streams, the brooks, the mists, the—er—fens, the—er—glens, by to-night's mail-train."

Not only was there no sign of Celia, but in an hour the banks would close. Wylie squeezed open the hands and hastened away. He had indeed to leave her, but not for long, for his tastes were expensive and Cooper had whispered that the Cox was dead. Miss Counihan followed slowly.

The Cox had swallowed 110 aspirins following the breaking off of a friendship with a Mr. Sacha Few, an anti-vivisection worker.

Neary and Cooper came out, closely followed by Dr. Killiecrankie, who locked the mortuary, fixed Cooper with his eye, pointed to the ground at his feet, said, " Be here in an hour ", and was gone.

Neary seeing Wylie afar off, Miss Counihan following slowly and no sign of Celia, said, " Dump it anywhere ", and hastened away.

Cooper called after him :

" She is dead."

Neary stopped but did not turn. He thought

for a second that Celia was meant. Then he
corrected himself and exulted.

"Some time," said Cooper.

Neary went on, Cooper stood looking after
him. Wylie having travelled twice as fast as
Miss Counihan, disappeared round the corner
of the main block. Miss Counihan turned,
saw Neary coming up behind her at a great
pace, stopped, then advanced slowly to meet
him. Neary tacked sharply, straightened up
when she made no move to cut him off and
passed her rapidly at a comfortable remove,
his hat raised in salute and his head averted.
Miss Counihan followed slowly.

Cooper did not know what had happened
to set him free of those feelings that for so many
years had forbidden him to take a seat or
uncover his head, nor did he pause to inquire.
He placed his ancient bowler crown upward
on the step, squatted high above it, took careful
aim through his crutch, closed his eye, set his
teeth, flung his feet forward into space and came
down on his buttocks with the force of a pile
ram. No second blow was necessary.

The furnace would not draw, it was past
five o'clock before Cooper got away from the
Mercyseat with the parcel of ash under his arm.
It must have weighed well on four pounds.

Various ways of getting rid of it suggested themselves to him on the way to the station. Finally he decided that the most convenient and inconspicuous was to drop it in the first considerable receptacle for refuse that he came to. In Dublin he need only have sat down on the nearest bench and waited. Soon one of the gloomy dustmen would have come, wheeling his cart marked, " Post your litter here." But London was less conscious of her garbage, she had not given her scavenging to aliens.

He was turning into the station, without having met any considerable receptacle for refuse, when a burst of music made him halt and turn. It was the pub across the way, opening for the evening session. The lights sprang up in the saloon, the doors burst open, the radio struck up. He crossed the street and stood on the threshold. The floor was palest ochre, the pin-tables shone like silver, the quoits board had a net, the stools the high rungs that he loved, the whiskey was in glass tanks, a slow cascando of pellucid yellows. A man brushed past him into the saloon, one of the millions that had been wanting a drink for the past two hours. Cooper followed slowly and sat down at the bar, for the first time in more than twenty years.

" What are you taking, friend ? " said the man.

" The first is mine," said Cooper, his voice trembling.

Some hours later Cooper took the packet of ash from his pocket, where earlier in the evening he had put it for greater security, and threw it angrily at a man who had given him great offence. It bounced, burst, off the wall on to the floor, where at once it became the object of much dribbling, passing, trapping, shooting, punching, heading and even some recognition from the gentleman's code. By closing time the body, mind and soul of Murphy were freely distributed over the floor of the saloon ; and before another dayspring greyened the earth had been swept away with the sand, the beer, the butts, the glass, the matches, the spits, the vomit.

13

LATE afternoon, Saturday, October the 26th. A mild, clear, sunless day, sudden gentle eddies of rotting leaves, branches still against the still sky, from a chimney a pine of smoke.

Celia wheeled Mr. Willoughby Kelly south along the Broad Walk. He wore his kiting costume, a glistening slicker many sizes too large for him and a yachting-cap many sizes too small, though the smallest and largest of their kind obtainable. He sat bolt upright, with one gloved hand clutching the winch, with the other the kite furled and in its sheath, and his blue eyes blazed in the depths of their sockets. To either side of him the levers flailed the air with heavy strokes, causing a light draught that he found not unpleasant, for he burned with excitement.

At the top of the incline he laid the winch and kite in his lap and seized the pulls. It was the signal for Celia to let go. His arms flashed back and forth, faster and faster as the

chair gathered speed, until he was rocking
crazily along at a good 12 m.p.h., a danger
to himself and to others. Then resisting with
one hand the pull, with the other the thrust
of the levers, he brought himself smoothly to
rest level with the statue of Queen Victoria,
whom he greatly admired, as a woman and as
a queen.

It was only in the legs and face that Mr.
Kelly was badly gone, he still had plenty of
vigour in his arms and torso.

He was as fond of his chair in his own way as
Murphy had been of his.

Celia was a long time coming. He unwrapped
the old silk kite, stained and faded hexagon of
crimson, stretched it on its asterisk of sticks,
made fast the tail and line, tested the tassels
one by one. One just such milky Saturday
afternoon many years previously a regular had
said : " Silk ain't worth a b——. Give me nainsook." To which Mr. Kelly recalled with satisfaction the exact terms of his rejoinder, which
had been loudly applauded : " Nainsook my
rump."

Celia touched the back of his chair and he
said :

" You were a long time."

" Business," said Celia.

The leaves began to lift and scatter, the higher branches to complain, the sky broke and curdled over flecks of skim blue, the pine of smoke toppled into the east and vanished, the pond was suddenly a little panic of grey and white, of water and gulls and sails.

It was as though Time suddenly lost patience, or had an anxiety attack.

Beyond the Long Water Rosie Dew and Nelly, the worst of her heat behind her, turned their faces to the rising wind and home. A pair of socks was waiting from Lord Gall. He had written : " If this pair of socks does not prove more productive, I shall have to try a new control."

Celia wheeled Mr. Kelly into position, at the north-east corner of the plot between the Round Pond and the Broad Walk, the prow of his chair wedged against the railing. She took the assembled kite gently from his hands, backed along the path until she stood on the margin of the water, held up the kite as high as her arms would reach and waited for the glove to fall. The wind blew her skirt against her legs, her jacket back from her breasts. A week-end lecher well advanced in years, sprawling on his sacrum (which was a mass of eczema) in a chair directly before her, discomposed his features in what he had good reason to suppose was the smile obscene, and jingled his change, his very small change. Celia smiled back, strained upward with her arms, settled herself more firmly on the ground.

Mr. Kelly's hand felt the wind he wanted, the glove fell, Celia threw up the kite. And so great was his skill that in five minutes he was lying back, breathing hard and short, his eyes closed of necessity but in ecstasy as it happened, half his line paid out, sailing by feel.

Celia paused for a second to clinch the client, then rejoined Mr. Kelly. The cord wormed slowly off the winch—out, back a little, stop ; out, back a little, stop. The historical process of the hardened optimists. With still a quarter of the line to go the kite rode without a flicker high above the Dell, a speck in the glades that this wind always opened in the east. The chair drove against the railing, Mr. Kelly wished his bottom were more prehensile. Without opening his eyes he said :

" You did that very nicely."

Celia did not choose to misunderstand him.

" And yesterday ? " said Mr. Kelly.

" A kid and a drunk," said Celia.

Mr. Kelly let out a wild rush of line, say the

industrial revolution, then without recoil or stop, gingerly, the last few feet. The kite being now absolutely at the end of its tether, he sat up and opened his eyes, hypermetropic in the extreme, to admire the effect.

Except for the sagging soar of line, undoubtedly superb so far as it went, there was nothing to be seen, for the kite had disappeared from view. Mr. Kelly was enraptured. Now he could measure the distance from the unseen to the seen, now he was in a position to determine the point at which seen and unseen met. It would be an unscientific observation, so many and so fitful were the imponderables involved. But the pleasure accruing to Mr. Kelly would be in no way inferior to that conferred (presumably) on Mr. Adams by his beautiful deduction of Neptune from Uranus. He fixed with his eagle eyes a point in the empty sky where he fancied the kite to swim into view, and wound carefully in.

Moving away a little Celia also looked at the sky, not with the same purpose as Mr. Kelly, for she knew that he would see it long before she could, but simply to have that unction of soft sunless light on her eyes that was all she remembered of Ireland. Gradually she saw other kites, but above all the tandem of the child that had not answered her good night, because he had been singing. She recognised the unusual coupling, not in file but abreast.

/ The ludicrous fever of toys struggling skyward, the sky itself more and more remote, the wind tearing the awning of cloud to tatters, pale limitless blue and green recessions laced with strands of scud, the light failing—once she would have noticed these things. She watched the tandem coming shakily down from the turmoil, the child running forward to break its fall, his trouble when he failed, his absorbed kneeling over the damage. He did not sing as he departed, nor did she hail him.

The wail of the rangers came faintly out of the east against the wind. *All out. All out. All out.* Celia turned and looked at Mr. Kelly. He lay back sideways in the chair, his cheek on his shoulder, a fold of the slicker lifting his lip in a mild snarl, not dying but dozing. As she watched the winch sprang from his fingers, struck violently against the railing, the string snapped, the winch fell to the ground, Mr. Kelly awoke.

All out. All out.

Mr. Kelly tottered to his feet, tossed up his arms high and wide and quavered away down the path that led to the water, a ghastly, lamentable figure. The slicker trailed along the ground, the skull gushed from under the cap like a dome from under its lantern, the ravaged face was a cramp of bones, throttled sounds jostled in his throat.

Celia caught him on the margin of the pond. The end of the line skimmed the water, jerked upward in a wild whirl, vanished joyfully in the dusk. Mr. Kelly went limp in her arms. Someone fetched the chair and helped to get him aboard. Celia toiled along the narrow path into the teeth of the wind, then faced north up the wide hill. There was no shorter way home. The yellow hair fell across her face. The yachting-cap clung like a clam to the skull. The levers were the tired heart. She closed her eyes.

All out.